ASHLEY FARLEY

RETURN TO MARSH HOLLOW

Soul Seekers

Also By Ashley Farley

Sandy Island

Southern Discomfort

Beneath the Carolina Sun

Southern Simmer

Marsh Point

Long Journey Home

Echoes of the Past

Songbird's Second Chance

Heart of Lowcountry

After the Storm

Scent of Magnolia

Virginia Vineyards

Love Child

Blind Love

Forbidden Love

Love and War

Palmetto Island

Muddy Bottom

Change of Tides

Lowcountry on My Mind

Sail Away

Scottie's Adventures

Breaking the Story

Merry Mary

One

2008

Tears well in my eyes as I raise my glass to toast the only true friends I've ever known. "To Giorgio and Carmela—wishing you Godspeed as you ride off into the sunset to live out your golden years in Maui." My voice wavers. I lower my gaze, swiping at my eyes dangerously close to an ugly cry.

I've been fighting back emotion throughout this bon voyage lunch. After twenty-two years of waitressing at Bella Tavola, I'm going to miss my friends as much as I'll miss the job.

Our staff of ten has polished off countless bottles of champagne, yet no one wants to leave. It's nearly four o'clock, but we're delaying the inevitable—the final goodbye. We'll part with promises to visit, but we know the truth. Frequent visits don't happen when an ocean and an entire country lie between you.

Giorgio and Carmela searched for months for a buyer for the business. But trendy new spots with craft cocktails and small plates have taken over, leaving old-school Italian restaurants like ours in the dust. Nostalgia doesn't stand a chance against modern dining trends.

When someone suggests moving the party to a hot spot down the street, I take it as my cue to leave. I push back from the table. "I'm out! I need to get home."

To my empty house and bleak future.

"I'll help you get your things," Carmela says, rising slowly and walking with me to the break room.

I empty my locker into a canvas tote bag—an old order pad, a crumpled box of peppermint tea, a flattened protein bar, and my favorite cashmere scarf. "I thought I'd lost this," I say, wrapping the scarf around my neck.

I close the locker and turn to face Carmela. "I hate goodbyes."

"Me too." She cups my cheek. "But this isn't goodbye, sweetheart. You'll come for a visit as soon as we get settled in Maui."

I smile, but a strange ache tells me I might never see my beloved friend again.

Carmela presses an envelope in my hand. "This is for you."

"What's this?" I ask, staring at it.

"A farewell bonus," she says, casting a nervous glance toward the dining room. "We didn't do this for the others, so keep it between us. We got an offer on the building last night, and we wanted you to have a little cushion . . . in case you decide to pursue your art career."

"I can't take this. I'm too old to be starting over. And you need the money for Hawaii." When I try to give the envelope back, Carmela gently pushes it away.

"You're never too old to chase your dreams, Lydia. Whether it's art lessons or a trip around the world, do something nice for yourself for a change."

The stubborn set of her jaw tells me not to argue. "Thanks," I murmur, tucking the envelope in my pocket. I wrap my arms around her in a tight hug. "Be safe, my friend."

My throat closes, and I rush out the kitchen's back door before I lose it completely.

A burst of invigorating spring air greets me as I step outside. I pause on the concrete delivery platform, inhaling deeply, exhaling slowly—steadying my breath. Digging through my tote, I find a tissue, blow my nose, and follow the brick-lined alley around the building to the sidewalk.

The sun warms my face as I stroll through Richmond's quaint Fan District toward home. Summer will be here soon, bringing the long, sultry days I both anticipate and dread. It's the only time I let myself think about my childhood on the Chesapeake Bay—the salt-kissed air, the marshes. But even those memories are shadowed by my tyrannical mother.

I'm a block away from the restaurant when Brandy catches up to me. "Lydia! Wait! You left without saying goodbye."

I dab at my eyes. "Sorry. I'm so emotional today. I had to leave before I turned into a blubbering mess."

"I know what you mean. It's a full-on cryfest in there now." She glances back toward the restaurant. "We haven't worked together long, but thank you . . . for being a good friend to me when I needed one."

Carmela had refused to hire the runaway teen when she first showed up, looking for a job. But I saw something of myself in her and convinced Carmela to give Brandy a chance.

I squeeze her arm. "I'm so proud of you for overcoming your problems."

"I'm not there yet," Brandy says, her eyes brimming. "But I'm trying."

I pull her in for a hug. "Oh, honey. Just take it one day at a time."

"But I can't find a job," she sobs. "And my rent's due soon."

I rub slow circles on her back. "Have you thought about going home?"

Brandy nods against my shoulder. "Do you think my parents will forgive me?"

"You never know until you try. I imagine they'd be thrilled to see how far you've come."

"Maybe," she whispers. "I was such a mess back then. I wouldn't blame them if they never speak to me again." She steps back, wiping her tears with her jacket sleeve. "Can we stay in touch?"

I smile. "I'd love that. You know where to find me if you need anything."

"Bye, Lydia," she says, her head low as she turns to walk away.

"Bye, Brandy," I call after her. "Chin up!"

I watch Brandy disappear into the crowd at the bus stop before continuing toward home. When I reach my front steps, I dig through my tote for my keys, too distracted to notice the gentleman sitting on my front porch swing—until he speaks.

"Afternoon."

"Oh!" I clutch my chest, my heart pounding. "I didn't see you there."

He rises off the swing, unfolding his long limbs with an easy grace. "I'm sorry. I didn't mean to startle you. Are you Lydia Meyer?"

"I am," I reply, eyeing him warily. He's attractive, his hair more salt than pepper, his suit impeccably tailored—a stark contrast to my weather-worn porch. "Can I help you with something?"

He steps down off the porch to the sidewalk, offering his hand. "Arthur Pendleton. I'm an attorney representing your mother's estate."

I blink, confused. "Did you say *my mother's estate*? Is she . . ." The words catch in my throat.

"I'm sorry to be the bearer of bad news. She passed away several months ago. We had the devil of a time locating you."

I swallow hard, the news knocking the breath from my lungs. "What happened to her?"

"The medical examiner's report lists the cause of death as natural. Old age, in other words."

"*Old age*?" I blink. "But she was only sixty-four."

Mama had me when she was twenty-six. I'm thirty-seven. The numbers add up. The medical examiner's report doesn't.

"If you'd like, I can put you in touch with someone who knows more about the circumstances of her death." He glances past me to my next-door neighbor, who's openly sweeping the same spot on her porch while blatantly eaves-dropping.

"Let's go inside, where we can talk in private." I lead him into the modest living room, quickly straightening pillows and folding the throw blanket I'd left crumpled on the sofa the night before.

"Please, have a seat. Can I offer you something—coffee, tea?"

He smiles, flashing a set of too-perfect teeth, likely crowns. "I'm fine, thank you."

Pendleton sits on the sofa, and I lower myself into an armchair opposite him, heart racing. My mind spins with questions, but I can't decide which one to ask first.

"My mother and I were estranged," I begin slowly. "I don't understand what her death has to do with me."

"She died without a will." He removes a bundle of docu-ments from his leather satchel. "Which means her estate passes to her children. All of it."

I take the papers, flipping through them without really seeing. "What about my sister, Melanie? She's two years older than me. Doesn't she get first dibs?"

"In cases like these, the estate is equally divided. But I've already spoken to Melanie. She has formally disclaimed her inheritance."

I pause, eyebrows raised. "I didn't realize that was an option, but count me in. I have no interest in a dilapidated house in the middle of nowhere."

He leans forward. "That *dilapidated house* sits on a hundred acres of prime waterfront real estate. I'm not sure when you last visited, but the surrounding peninsulas are now dotted with million-dollar homes."

"Then sell it. Let someone else build their dream home."

Pendleton clasps his hands over his knee. "On a hundred acres, a developer wouldn't build a dream home. He'd build several. But whether you sell is entirely up to you."

I close my eyes as memories I've worked hard to forget rise to the surface.

"I can't go back there," I whisper. "I won't survive it."

"If you disclaim," he says, carefully, "the estate passes to your son, Nathan."

My eyes snap open. "What about Melanie's children?"

"She doesn't have any," Mr. Pendleton says.

That surprises me. Melanie had always talked about having a house full of children. What happened? Was she unable to conceive? And if so, why didn't she adopt?

"I can see this has come as a shock to you, Miss Meyer. Take a few days to think it over. I'm available if you have questions." He slides a business card from his wallet and hands it to me. "You can reach me at any of the numbers listed on this card."

He pauses at the door, his hand resting lightly on the doorframe. "It's understandable to have mixed emotions about returning after so long. But seeing it again might give you clarity."

I remain seated long after the attorney leaves. Dusk creeps across the room, and I switch on the table lamp beside me. But I don't get up.

Arthur Pendleton has stirred something I haven't let myself feel in years—grief, guilt, dread, regret.

Mama may be gone, but Aurelia Meyer still has a powerful hold over me.

Two

I spend three days tackling long-overdue chores. After deep cleaning the house, I repair a broken porch rocker, purge three overstuffed closets, and haul a carload of donations to Goodwill. But by Wednesday morning, I can no longer avoid the most daunting project on my list—converting my son's room into an art studio.

It's not just about moving Nate's belongings to the basement storage room. He moved out after high school graduation four years ago, and with his own apartment a few miles away in Scott's Addition, he has no reason to stay the night here.

This is something else entirely. It's a shift. A turning point. And maybe, a quiet reckoning. Because once I claim this space as my own, I'll have no more excuses—nothing left to hide behind—to keep me from chasing the dream I tucked away decades ago.

As a girl, I used to paint for hours—landscapes, wildlife, the delicate beauty of the marshes and meadows surrounding Marsh Hollow. But when I left home, I left that part of myself behind too.

Over the years, I've amassed a small fortune in art supplies —tubes of paint, pristine brushes, blank canvases, and stacks of sketch pads. But I've yet to put brush to canvas.

What if I move everything into the sunniest room in the house and still can't find the courage—or inspiration—to paint?

My savings will cover my bills for a few months, giving me a soft landing before I need to look for a new job. Still, the real risk isn't financial.

As I brush my teeth, I mumble to my reflection in the mirror—mouth full of toothpaste, eyes full of doubt. "It's now or never, Liddy. You'll never know until you try."

But first—caffeine and breakfast.

With little to choose from in my refrigerator, I dress in exercise clothes and leave the house on foot. As it has every day since the attorney stopped by, my conversation with him weighs on my mind during the short walk to the Village Café. He unlocked something in me—a memory vault I didn't know was sealed. Now, snippets of my childhood flash before me at every turn. Some are pleasant. Most are not. Together, they form a fragmented picture of my youth—a story with missing pieces. Time, instead of providing clarity, has sharpened the gaps, bringing into focus the things I missed or chose to ignore. The harder I try to fit the pieces together, the more I realize how much of the puzzle is still missing.

Entering the cafe, I'm surprised to see Brandy sitting alone in a booth, a large suitcase on wheels upright beside her. She waves me over, and I slide onto the bench opposite her.

"Good morning. Are you going somewhere?" I ask, eyeing her suitcase.

Brandy drops her chin to her chest, slowly shaking her head. "A homeless shelter, maybe? My landlord kicked me out, and I have nowhere to go."

I reach across the table for her hand. "Oh, honey. I'm so sorry. Have you been to see your parents?"

"Yeah. They refuse to give me another chance. They're glad I'm doing better, but they don't think it's been long enough. They're afraid if they let me come home now, I'll slip back into my old ways."

"Do they know you lost your apartment? Aren't they worried about you living on the streets?"

Brandy shrugs. "I guess not. I just spent my last dollar on coffee." She lifts the mug to her lips, draining the rest of the coffee. "And now I have nothing left."

"Can you stay with a friend?"

Brandy fidgets with the sugar packets, her shoulders slumped. "I ran all my friends off. They got tired of taking care of me—of cleaning up my puke and covering for me with my parents."

I sit up straighter, lifting my chin. "Then you're coming home with me. I have a spare bedroom. You can stay with me until you get back on your feet." The words tumble out before I can stop them, offering the perfect excuse to postpone turning the spare room into my art studio.

"Thanks, but that's asking too much," Brandy says, dabbing at her eyes with a napkin.

"You're not asking. I'm insisting."

She lowers the napkin from her face, searching my expression. "Really? Do you mean it? It would only be for a short time. I can sleep on your sofa. Or even your floor."

I chuckle. "Don't be silly. You'll stay in my spare room. Now, let's order some breakfast. My treat." I slide a menu across the table to her.

Brandy hesitates, glancing down at the menu. "Are you sure? I can pay you back. But I am kinda hungry."

"I'm positive. And you don't have to pay me back. Order whatever you want."

We both go for the breakfast special, and as we eat, Brandy tells me about the many jobs she's applied for—waitressing, bartending, even clerking at Libbie Market, a neighborhood gourmet store.

"Good for you, Brandy. You've made good use of your time. Something will turn up soon," I say, taking the last bite of scrambled eggs.

"I hope so." Brandy crunches a slice of bacon. "What about you, Lydia? Have you found a job yet?"

"I was planning to take some time off to paint—an old hobby of mine . . ." My voice trails off as thoughts of Marsh Hollow push their way in, uninvited.

Brandy tilts her head, studying me. "I hear a *but* in there. What aren't you telling me?"

I push my empty plate away. "Something has come up that's making me rethink my plans."

A line forms between Brandy's brows. "That doesn't sound good. Is something wrong? You're not in any kind of trouble, are you?"

I lower my gaze. "It's nothing like that. It's just . . ."

"Just what? You can talk to me, Lydia. I've certainly dumped enough of my problems on you."

I smooth out my paper napkin, folding it into a small square. "I just found out my mother passed away."

Brandy's face falls. "Oh gosh. I'm so sorry. That must be so hard for you."

"Actually, we were estranged. I haven't seen her in a very long time. An attorney came to see me about her estate the other day." I tell Brandy about my dilemma.

"What're you gonna do?"

"My sister—my only sibling—has already disclaimed her share of the estate. I'm considering doing the same."

Brandy's eyes widen. "Disclaim it? But isn't that like giving away money?"

My shoulders sag. "My childhood was . . . *Unconventional* is the best way to describe it. I'm not sure I'm up to facing those old ghosts at Marsh Hollow."

"Seriously? You're the strongest person I know. You can handle anything. If you need me to, I'll go with you."

I reward Brandy's generous offer with a smile. "That's awfully kind of you, but I'm still thinking things through," I say, hoping to change the conversation.

The ringing of my cell phone in my purse provides the diversion I was looking for. I flip open the phone, but I don't recognize the number. "I'm not sure who this is, but I should answer it."

Brandy nods. "Of course. Go ahead."

When I answer the call, the attorney's booming baritone fills the line. "Miss Meyer, Arthur Pendleton here. I apologize for calling so soon after I promised to give you time to contemplate your mother's estate, but a situation has arisen that you should be aware of."

I glance over at Brandy, who is busy examining the split ends of her auburn hair. "Yes, sir. Give me a minute, please. I'm in the middle of something."

"Take your time," Pendleton replies.

I press the phone to my chest. "I need to take this. When the waitress comes back, give her this." I hand Brandy my credit card and hurry out of the cafe.

"What is it, Mr. Pendleton? Is something wrong?"

"On the contrary. A real estate developer has made a handsome offer on your property," he says, then tells me the amount.

I freeze. "That's a lot of money, Mr. Pendleton."

"Indeed, it is. But the property is worth it, which is why I cautioned you not to be hasty in disclaiming. I'm not a Realtor, Miss Meyer. I recommend hiring one if you decide to proceed."

I stare at my reflection in the cafe window, my blue-green eyes wide, my blonde bob grazing my shoulders. This just got real.

"What did you tell the developer?"

"That you're still in shock over your mother's death and need time to process. He's giving you until the end of May to respond."

"The end of May?" I scoff. "That's only five weeks away!"

"I'm sure he'll grant an extension, if necessary, but you can't delay indefinitely." A moment of silence stretches between us. "Since your sister disclaimed her share, I'm not obligated to call her—unless you'd like me to."

I hesitate. "Not yet. I may try calling her myself. I'll get back to you by the end of the week."

When I end the call, I look up to find Brandy watching me suspiciously.

"Everything okay?" she asks.

I pocket my phone. "Yes! Just my mother's estate attorney pressuring me to visit Marsh Hollow." I notice Brandy's suitcase at her side. "Shall we go?"

Her face lights up. "Whenever you're ready!"

We walk for a while in silence, my mind stuck on Brandy's earlier comment. *Isn't that like giving away money?* The amount of money the developer offered could feed all the starving children in Africa for a decade. Someone needs to look into the matter. And since Mellie has stated her position, that someone is me.

"What's all this?" Brandy asks when she sees the neatly stacked art supplies occupying one corner of my living room.

"Art supplies. They've waited this long. They'll wait another day. Who knows, I may never start painting again," I say, suddenly feeling empty inside.

Brandy leaves her suitcase at the door and walks to the

corner, kneeling to examine the supplies. "Why did you ever stop?"

I cross my arms. "Lack of inspiration, I guess. Nothing has ever moved me the way the marsh and meadows of Marsh Hollow did. I can still see them vividly in my mind, but I can't seem to transfer them to canvas. It's like writer's block for artists."

"Hmm." Brandy removes the cover from a set of acrylic paints. "How long has it been since you were last there?"

"Twenty-two years."

"Whoa. That's a long time. Even if those visions still *feel* vivid, it's natural for them to have faded over time. Maybe seeing them in person will bring them back to life."

A flicker of hope stirs in my chest, but it's fleeting. "I can't. I told you—there are too many painful memories there."

Brandy studies me, her expression unreadable. "You say that, but I can tell you're thinking about going there."

"Am I?" I ask, brushing a paintbrush absently against my cheek.

"Yep." She straightens. "These canvases won't paint themselves. Don't you have a spare bedroom you can use as a studio?"

I don't have an answer. Brandy reads the guilt on my face.

"Oh. I get it. You promised that room to me." She waves it off. "Seriously, Lydia. I'll be fine on the sofa."

"Absolutely not. I won't hear of it. Now, let me show you your room." I motion her to the steps, pushing away thoughts of Marsh Harbor . . . for now.

Three

1978

I was only seven, and Melanie just two years older, when Mama left us alone overnight for the first time.

We were picking strawberries on a warm April afternoon when Mama came to tell us she was leaving. Shielding my eyes from the sun, I looked up at her. She wore jeans, worn work boots, and a blue-checked blouse, her thick auburn hair trailing in a single braid beneath a denim bucket hat.

"When y'all finish picking berries, divide them in the containers, and I'll take them to market tomorrow."

"Yes, ma'am," we answered in unison.

Mama turned to Mellie. "Walk with me to the truck. I need to talk to you about something important."

"Yes, ma'am," Mellie said, scrambling to her feet.

I watched curiously as my sister followed Mama down the rows of crops, kicking at the gravel in the driveway while Mama spoke to her beside the truck.

"What'd she say?" I asked Mellie when she returned.

Mellie shrugged, her bare shoulders tanned golden brown by the sun. "Nothing important."

But I knew better. My sister only lied when the truth was too much to bear.

It took us until late afternoon to finish picking the strawberries. Hauling the heavy buckets back to the house, we filled the purple cardboard containers with berries and neatly arranged them in wooden crates on the screened-in back porch.

I wiped the sweat from my eyes, glancing around. "Mama's not back yet. What're we supposed to do now?"

Mellie grinned, tossing her arms wide. "Anything we want. We have the whole farm to ourselves."

I bounced on my toes. "Goody! Can we go to the marsh?"

"Sorry, kiddo." Mellie's voice carried the smooth authority of someone much older than two years. "I promised Mama we'd stay away from the water. Let's explore the woods." Her gaze shifted to the dense stand of pine trees beyond the fields.

A shiver of unease crept up my spine. "But we're not allowed."

"Mama's not here. She'll never know. We'll only go as far as the stream," Mellie said, that mischievous glint sparkling in the golden flecks of her hazel eyes.

My stomach churned. Going along with my sister's mischief usually ended in punishment. "What stream?"

"Come on. I'll show you." Mellie took off across the field, laughter trailing behind her like a dare.

I hesitated. The woods had always seemed off-limits for a reason, but staying alone at the house felt even scarier. With a deep breath, I ran after her, my feet pounding the earth as I raced to keep up.

"How do you know there's a stream in the woods?" I asked, eyeing the only known entrance through the tangled underbrush.

Mellie smirked. "Because at night, I hear water rolling over rocks through our open window."

I shot her a skeptical look. "I sleep in the bed beside you. How come I never hear it?"

"Because you sleep like a bear in the winter." Mellie pulled a low-hanging branch aside and took a tentative step into the shadows. "Are you coming?"

I sucked in an unsteady breath. "Yes. But I don't like it."

Crouching low, I stayed close as we crept along a narrow, overgrown path. The air was thick, damp, and cool, a stark contrast to the golden spring afternoon we'd left behind. My teeth began to chatter—not from the chill but from the prickling fear curling in my gut. Twigs and branches clawed at my bare arms and legs like unseen hands, urging me to turn back. Overhead, an owl hooted, the eerie sound stretching through the trees like a warning. We didn't belong here.

I tugged on the hem of Mellie's shirt. "I don't hear any stream. Let's go back."

Mellie reached back for my hand. "There's nothing to be afraid of, Liddy. There's only one path. We can't get lost."

I sighed. "Ugh. Okay," I said, my fingers wrapping firmly around hers.

We moved cautiously, our bare feet rustling against damp leaves. After a short distance, Mellie called softly over her shoulder, "I see daylight up ahead. Maybe it's the stream."

Around the next bend, we stumbled upon a small clearing enclosed by a wrought-iron fence. Its black bars were laced with creeping vines, the heavy gate stood slightly ajar, as though inviting us in—or daring us to enter. A hush descended over the space, as though the trees themselves were holding their breath.

"What is it?" I asked, pressing myself against my sister's side.

"Looks like a graveyard." Mellie peeled me off of her and opened the heavy gate. "You stay here. I'm going to check it out."

"No! Wait!" I cried, but Mellie was already inside.

My fingers curled around the top of the gate as I watched my sister weave through the small space. When she knelt to inspect something on the ground, my stomach clenched. "What is it? What do you see?"

Mellie pressed her finger to her lips. "Shh! Keep your voice down. I'll be out in a minute."

I glanced around nervously. There was no one here to hear us, except maybe the dead beneath our feet.

Mellie lingered in the graveyard for what felt like an eternity. When she finally emerged, the buoyant energy she'd carried earlier was gone. Her face was pale, her shoulders stiff. She looked troubled, maybe even afraid.

"What's in there?" I asked, my voice barely above a whisper.

"A bunch of graves with our last name on them. Some of them were babies." She pauses. "And this creepy statue, a weird-looking man."

My eyes widened. "There's a man in the cemetery?"

"No, dummy. The statue *is* a man. His name is Ambrose Malone. What kinda name is Ambrose?" She swung the gate shut behind us. "You can never tell Mama we were here."

I drew an *X* over my chest. "I promise! Cross my heart and hope to die."

"Don't even say that," Mellie snapped, her voice sharp.

We walked hand in hand in silence back to the house. My stomach twisted when I saw the driveway empty. "Mama should be home by now. Did something happen to her?" My voice wavered, terror creeping in. Was she buried in one of those graves?

"She's not coming back until tomorrow. That's what she told me in the driveway before she left."

My lower lip trembled. "But who's gonna stay with us?"

"No one. We're fine by ourselves," Mellie grumbled.

"But I'm hungry. Who will make us dinner?" Tears spilled over my lids and rolled down my cheeks.

Mellie sighed, her tone softening. "Don't cry, Liddy. We'll have fun. Potato chip sandwiches for dinner with popsicles for dessert."

A coyote howled in the distance. My fingers gripped the hem of my dress. "I'm scared, Mellie."

Fear flashed in Mellie's eyes, but her voice remained calm. "We'll be fine. Let's go inside," she said, as she gently shoved me toward the kitchen door.

"Where did Mama go anyway?" I perched on a stool, my wide eyes following her hands as she crumbled potato chips between slices of bread.

"She's at work." Mellie sliced the sandwich in half.

"But I thought she worked in the barn," I said, referring to the small office where we were forbidden to go.

"She does. Now stop asking so many questions and eat your sandwich." She set a plate in front of me with a thud.

Tears stung my eyes. I hated it when my sister was mean. And her bad mood lingered after dinner as she read to me, and when we got ready for bed.

"Are you mad at me, Mellie?" I asked finally, curled up in my twin bed.

"Of course not, Liddy. Now go to sleep." Mellie switched off the bedside table lamp, plunging the room into darkness.

Sometime in the night, Mellie cried out, jolting me awake. I rushed to her bedside, my heart hammering. "Mellie! Mellie! Wake up. You're having a bad dream."

Mellie bolted upright, her eyes wild, sweat glistening on her face.

"Are you okay?" I whispered. "What were you dreaming about?"

She pressed her hands to her eyes. "The cemetery in the woods. The souls of all those dead people—" A shudder

19

wracked her slight frame. "They're inside me. I can hear them. They're gonna make me do bad things. And that man . . . that statue . . . He said he'll hurt me if I disobey the souls."

"It was just a dream." I nudged her over and climbed into bed beside her, pulling the blankets over both of us. "You're safe. I won't let anything happen to you."

Mellie sniffled and rolled onto her side. "It felt so real."

"I know." I wrapped an arm around her, curling up behind her. "But it's not real. I promise."

The room fell quiet, the only sound the soft hum of the fan in the corner. Mellie's breathing slowed, but I stayed awake, my eyes fixed on the shadows stretching across the ceiling. I held my sister a little closer, as if that could keep the nightmares and the woods at bay.

Four

2008

I jolt awake, the remnants of my dream clinging to me like cobwebs—fleeting images of charcoal smudges, crumpled paper, and Mama's disapproving frown. In the distance, behind it all, the cemetery looms.

Once I started drawing, I couldn't stop. I sketched everything in sight, as if the world might disappear unless I captured it on paper. I was obsessed. I knew I had talent—and I'm certain Mama knew it too, though she never said so. My art became our battleground, a quiet war of wills. As I entered adolescence, my passion only deepened, but Mama's relentless determination to smother that spark always seemed to win out.

Realizing sleep won't come again, I slip out of bed, wrap myself in my robe, and pad downstairs to the kitchen. I don't turn on the light, relying instead on the soft green glow of the stove clock while I fumble to make coffee.

Seated at the kitchen table with the steaming mug in front of me, I finally give in to the pull of my memories.

In an abandoned trunk tucked into the far corner of the attic, I used to keep my sketches and meager art supplies—

scraps of paper, the pencils I used for schoolwork, and the set of children's watercolors I had purchased with my allowance money from the general store in Colton when Mama wasn't looking.

I picture myself standing at the attic window, overlooking the water, watching the birds gather in the marsh. The dream has stirred something in me—a need I haven't felt in years. A powerful, aching urge to create.

The first rays of dawn are creeping through the blinds, glinting off the white wooden tabletop, when Brandy enters the kitchen.

The girl startles and emits an audible gasp. "Geez, Lydia! You scared me. Why are you sitting in the dark?"

"Just reminiscing about the past. I've decided to go to Marsh Hollow for a visit," I say, the words slipping out before I can second-guess them. I press my fingers to my lips, barely believing what I've just said. Is that it? Have I made up my mind? Am I really going home to Marsh Hollow?

"Good for you!" Brandy dumps the last of the old coffee down the sink, then measures fresh grounds into the machine. "How long will you be gone?"

I shake my head. "I'm not sure. A couple of weeks at the most."

"Will you paint while you're there?" Brandy asks, retrieving a mug from the cabinet.

"I hope so. At least, I'm going to try. I think maybe you were right. The visions have faded. I need to experience them again in person to stir the inspiration. Will you be okay staying at my house by yourself?"

"Of course! I'll be fine. I can look after things for you."

"Great. I'll feel better knowing someone is in the house." Eager for fresh coffee, I get up and remove the cream from the refrigerator.

"When will you go?" Brandy asks, filling her mug with coffee.

"Today! As soon as I can pack. Before I change my mind." Hope flitters across my chest at the promise of an adventure. I can't remember the last time I left Richmond. A beach trip to the Lowcountry five years ago, maybe? This won't be a vacation but a . . . a change of scenery.

I snicker to myself. *A change of scenery?* The scenery I've longed to see for more than two decades.

Two hours later, I hoist my large suitcase into the back of my Highlander with my art supplies and slam the rear door. I turn to Brandy. "Take care of my house for me. And call if anything comes up."

"Will do. Don't worry about a thing. I promise, no wild parties," Brandy says with a mischievous glint in her eyes.

I drop my smile. Considering the girl's troubled past, am I doing the right thing by leaving my home in her care?

Brandy squeezes my shoulder. "Relax, Lydia. I'm only joking. You can count on me. I would never break your trust."

I exhale a breath I didn't realize I was holding. "I'm a little on edge. All these old memories are getting to me."

Brandy throws her arms around me. "That's only natural, but sometimes, the only way to lay old ghosts to rest is to face them head-on."

"True." Drawing away from her, I place my hand on Brandy's cheek. "How'd you get to be so smart at such a young age?"

"I learned a lot from you." Brandy opens the driver's side door. "You need to get on the road. And be sure to call me when you get there."

"Yes, ma'am." Slipping behind the wheel, I start the engine and ease away from the curb. Through the rearview mirror, I watch my house shrink into the distance, a bittersweet ache building in my chest. In my gut, I know—life won't be the same after this.

Twenty minutes later, I'm crossing the city limits, my mind on the trip ahead, when I realize I don't have a key to the house at Marsh Hollow. At the next stoplight, I punch in Arthur Pendleton's number, and he answers right away.

"Miss Meyer. I was hoping to hear from you."

"Good morning, Mr. Pendleton. I'm on my way to Marsh Hollow. I have no idea what I'll do when I get there or how long I'll stay. Do you have a key to get in the house?"

"I'll have my associate leave one for you under the mat." He coughs, clearing his throat. "I should warn you—the house needs some work."

"The house I remember could use a bulldozer."

"And that might very well be what it gets. At the very least, you'll need to do a thorough cleaning to make it habitable."

What is he not telling me? I decide not to press. I've only just gotten one leg over the fence, and the last thing I need is someone yanking me back down. Whatever state the house is in, I'll deal with it. "Thanks for the heads-up. I'll stop for cleaning supplies on the way."

"Okay, then. I'll check in with you in a few days. My office is in Colton, right around the corner, should you need anything."

I feel oddly invigorated as I end the call, set the cruise control, and turn up the volume on my country music station. Brandy was right. Instead of running from my childhood, I need to make peace with it, to lay those old ghosts to rest. The past isn't something I can erase. It's as much a part of me as my skin.

The memories, both tender and painful, are etched into me like faint freckles or deep lines, shaping the person I've become.

While the small town of Colton has grown in my absence, it has retained much of its coastal charm. Car dealerships and big-box stores greet me on the outskirts of town, but once I get to Main Street, very little has changed. I pass The Creamery Cove where we went for ice cream on special occasions like birthdays. Mama made most of our clothes, but we purchased our shoes from Mariner's Mercantile, along with supplies for school, the kitchen, and the farm.

I locate a parking spot and enter Tidewater Grocery. Memories flash in my mind as I wander the aisles. Mellie and me hiding behind displays of Quaker Oats and Aunt Jemima pancake mix while spying on the town children shopping with their mamas—little girls in pretty dresses with satin ribbons in their hair and little boys in baseball uniforms.

Mellie, whose fascination with the children bordered on obsessive, pestered Mama with questions on the way home from town. "Why can't we be like normal kids? I hate living on a farm. Can't we please move to town? I want to go to a real school like everyone else." Mellie's relentless questions often pushed Mama too far, usually ending with us being sent to bed without dinner.

I quickly gather enough provisions and supplies to last a few days—coffee, eggs, the ingredients for salads, and a variety of cleaning solutions.

From Colton, I drive another thirty minutes to the farm. The entrance to Marsh Hollow is nearly swallowed by overgrown brush, and I drive past it the first time. The forest has crept in on the gravel driveway, tree branches scraping against my car in places. When the trees break apart, the house is visible, weathered and worn, standing at the edge of dandelion-covered fields. Beyond it, the creek stretches wide, spilling into the Chesapeake Bay, its waters shimmering under the afternoon light. My breath catches, and my foot slams on the brake pedal.

The memories come fast and furious as I turn off the engine and step out of the car—Mellie and me as young children, flying kites, building snowmen, and chasing a scraggly puppy. What was that puppy's name? Gypsy! We never knew where she came from. She just wandered onto the farm one day, and Mama reluctantly agreed to let us keep her. But then Gypsy ate an entire loaf of homemade bread off the counter, and by morning, she was gone. While we never found out for sure what happened to her, we suspected Mama had given her away or dropped her off at the pound.

Discouraged, I return to the car and continue down the driveway to the water side of the house—known as the front yard in the South. The house is in worst shape than I expected, with missing shutters and peeling siding in desperate need of paint. The railing is rotten, and the brick steps crumble beneath my feet as I climb up to the front porch.

As I'm locating the key from under the mat, a cool breeze tickles the back of my neck, sending chills down my spine and raising goose bumps on my arms. An eerie feeling washes over me. I glance around, my heart pounding. Is someone watching me? Is Mama still here?

Your mother is dead, Liddy, I remind myself as I jam the key into the lock with a trembling hand.

The door creaks open, but I freeze in the doorway, my pulse pounding in my ears. The living room has been ransacked. A chair lies overturned near the cold fireplace, stuffing spilling from its torn fabric. Papers litter the floor, scattered across the threadbare rug, as if someone had rifled through them and left in a hurry. I frown and kneel to pick up a brittle grocery list in Mama's neat cursive. Another, a crumpled note, has ink that has bled into an unreadable smear.

Paintings have been slashed and picture frames shattered,

the glass now scattered across the floor in glittering shards. The couch cushions have been slit open, their insides strewn across the room like snowdrifts of feathers and foam. One of Mama's old quilts lies in the corner, half-buried under debris, its once-vibrant patterns dulled with dust and grime. Someone has ripped through this house—not just rummaging, but tearing, ravaging, violating.

I push the debris aside with my foot and move toward the kitchen.

The cabinets hang open, doors askew, as if wrenched open with force. Broken dishes glint from the sink, their jagged edges reflecting the pale light filtering through the grime-streaked windows. The pantry door hangs off its hinges while empty shelves yawn behind it. Someone didn't just take what they wanted. They pulled everything apart, searching for something.

Then I see it—graffiti, scrawled on the wall in a deep crimson hue, an elaborate tangle of lines that is stark against the faded yellow paint. I can't tell what it is at first, but as I step closer, the design sharpens. The letters D and V emerge, entwined so intricately they seem to knot together.

A shudder rolls through me. What is DV? A gang? A message? A warning?

But what could anyone possibly want from a sixty-four-year-old midwife?

The medical examiner ruled her death natural—old age.

Could this be unrelated? Just senseless destruction? A random act of violence?

I want to believe that. Yet I can't shake the feeling someone came here looking for something. And they were desperate enough to destroy everything in their path.

But who? What were they after? And why Mama?

Unless . . . they broke in after she died.

Five

My first instinct is to run to my sister, just as I'd always done when something went wrong. But Mellie isn't here. She's disclaimed her inheritance, leaving me to deal with Mama's estate alone. Leaving me with this awful mess.

Backing out of the house, I close and lock the door behind me. This is too much, too overwhelming. I never should have come here. Hurrying to my car, I start the engine and tear out of the gravel driveway, away from the house and its suffocating memories.

I'm retreating past the dandelion fields when Mama's voice cuts through the silence, filling the car like an unwanted apparition. "*Coward! Go ahead, run away. You always were a fraidy cat.*"

I let go of the steering wheel and clamp my hands over my ears, Mama's voice echoing in my head. The car veers off the driveway, narrowly missing a dead dogwood tree. I slam on the brakes, throw the car out of gear, and slump over the steering wheel, trembling.

Mama used to call me *Fraidy Cat*. She made up a little rhyme.

Fraidy cat, fraidy cat,
Hiding under Mama's hat.
Scared of shadows, scared of light,
Won't come out till past midnight.

When someone calls you something long enough, you start to believe it and step into that role. Mama's insults shaped me, molded me into the person I am today. I've played it safe my entire adult life. Twenty-two years as a waitress. No friends outside of work. No risks, no chances. I'm even afraid to paint—the one thing I was ever truly passionate about.

If I don't face the destruction in that house, I'll never be able to face myself in the mirror again.

But first, I need some answers.

I pull out my phone and tap Pendleton's number. When he picks up, I don't even say hello.

"You said the house needs a thorough cleaning. The house isn't dirty, Mr. Pendleton. The place has been ransacked. There's graffiti on the wall—and not just any graffiti. It looks like a seal. And the cause of death you gave me? Natural causes? That doesn't make sense."

I don't stop to breathe. The questions fire out of me like rockets, fueled by adrenaline and confusion.

When I finally pause, Pendleton responds with maddening calm. "I'll have someone from the sheriff's office reach out to you."

My jaw drops. "That's it? You can't tell me anything?"

"I'd rather you hear it from an official," he says, his tone clipped.

My fingers grip the phone. "Am I even safe staying here?"

He pauses, long enough to make my stomach twist. "I believe so."

"But you're not sure." I sigh, dragging a hand through my

hair. "I don't understand, Mr. Pendleton. Why did you pressure me into coming here?"

"It's your birthright, your family obligation," he says, as if that settles it. "I couldn't bear to see the property fall into the wrong hands."

I palm the steering wheel in frustration. "Why me? Why not my sister? She's the oldest."

"For several reasons. She's in New York. You live in Virginia. She's running a large company. You currently don't have a job. She gave permission to cremate your mother without even asking what caused her death. You, at least, care what happened to her."

The hair on the back of my neck bristles. *How does he know I'm unemployed?* But that seems beside the point now.

"How much did you tell Mellie? Does she even know about the vandalism?"

"She does not," he replies evenly.

I slump back against the car seat. Getting information out of him is like squeezing juice from a raisin. "Have someone from the sheriff's office call me as soon as possible," I say, then end the call before he can respond.

Driving slowly back to the house, I consider my options. Either stay or go home to Richmond. But Pendleton's voice keeps ringing in my head. *It's your birthright, your family obligation.*

I unload the grocery bags from the car and carry them into the kitchen, leaving them on the counter while I sweep up the trash and glass littering the floor. Despite the wreckage in the rest of the room, the pantry and refrigerator—ancient models from the 1960s—have been wiped clean. Not even a box of stale Triscuits or a moldy block of cheese remains. Either the *DV* gang members were really hungry, or someone cleared them out.

After organizing my purchases, I return to the car for my

suitcase. My footsteps slow as I climb the stairs, dread building with each one. At the top of the landing, on the right, awaits Mama's room. The door is closed. And closed it will stay.

In my room—and Mellie's—the damage isn't nearly as severe. Clothes and belongings left behind twenty-two years ago have been yanked from closets and drawers, strewn across the floor, and draped over the furniture. Nothing is broken. No pillows or mattresses slashed. But everything is covered in a thick layer of dust and grime.

I set to work, dusting and vacuuming and scrubbing. Two hours later, the air smells faintly of lemon and wood polish, sunlight filters through the clean windows, and my clothes are neatly tucked away.

Grateful for the warm weather, I toss together a salad and eat it at the picnic table on the back porch, mentally adding *replace screens* to my growing list of needed repairs. With the long evening stretching ahead, I set out to explore the waterfront, eager to reacquaint myself with the land that once felt like both home and prison.

The shoreline changed in my absence, now has a sandier beach and less grassy marsh. I don't remember the tide ever being this high. *Is the moon full now?*

In the ground on the bank of the hollow—a natural pond fed by a winding stream from the bay—I find the cross Mellie and I built years ago, fashioned from weathered stones we had painstakingly gathered one by one from around the property.

Mama turned faith into fear. Religion, for her, was about obedience, control, and punishment, not love or grace. But like so many other positive things in my life, my strong faith in God can be traced back to Mellie. My older sister taught me to trust in the Lord, to confide in Him whenever life became overwhelming. Even now, I say my prayers every night and rarely miss church on Sunday.

Dropping to my knees beside the primitive cross, I press

my hands together beneath my chin and close my eyes. *God, please grant me strength and guidance. I don't know what I'm doing. I'm scared to stay here, but something deeper is keeping me from walking away. I feel like an intruder in my own past— as if by leaving, I gave up the right to return. This was Mama's world, not mine. So why does it feel like I'm meant to be here now?*

I've heard stories on the news about gangs ransacking homes, but nothing like this has ever happened to anyone I know. Mama had nothing worth stealing. Seems like an awful lot of trouble to go through for a few spare dollars hidden in an old coffee can. Then again, junkies desperate for a fix have torn a place apart for far less.

I tackle the disarray on the first floor, hauling three carloads of trash to the dump. Mama had a phone installed while I was gone, but she stuck to her guns and never bought a television. Her chair in the living room is surrounded by stacks of books, most with their pages ripped out. The books alone make up an entire trip to the dump.

But there's still so much to do. Most of the upholstered furniture is ruined beyond repair. I'll need to hire someone to haul it off. I was joking when I mentioned a bulldozer to Mr. Pendleton, but now it seems like a reasonable option.

Tear down the house. Burn it. Burn it all.

Along with every horrid memory.

I'm sitting on the front steps, eyes fixed on the crumbling bricks beneath me, wondering why no one from the sheriff's office has called—trying to make sense of this mess—when a voice as smooth as midnight jazz drifts over me. "You're not giving up that easy, are you, Lydia?"

Startled, I jump to my feet, my heart racing. "Who are you? What're you doing on my property?"

"My name is Blossom, and you summoned me here."

I blink hard, taken aback. "I'm sorry, what? I don't remember calling anyone for help."

With flawless caramel skin and emerald eyes that seem to glow, the woman is almost too stunning to be real. But the mischievous smile playing on her lips, coupled with the mop of silver coils atop her head, makes her feel strangely familiar—comforting, even.

"Yesterday, when you visited the cross in the hollow, you asked God for strength and guidance. He sent me here to help you."

I rub my temples. "Great! First a crumbling house. Now a full-blown hallucination."

The woman offers a sympathetic smile. "You're not hallucinating, Lydia."

I frown. "How do you know my name?"

"I know lots of things about you, more than you may know yourself. Touch me if you don't believe I'm real," she says, holding out her hand. From her wrist dangles a single bracelet adorned with gold beads and a tiny cross made of what looks like mother-of-pearl.

I reach out tentatively, the tips of my fingers connecting with the back of her hand. A warmth unlike anything I've ever known wraps around me, stirring a quiet surge of hope and an inexplicable trust I can't explain. I only just met this woman, but I know beyond a shadow of a doubt I can count on her.

Suddenly confused by the intense connection, I quickly withdraw my hand. My gaze shifts from the woman's hand to her face. "What did you say your name was?"

"Blossom." She fingers a creamy petal of the gardenia bloom tucked into her mass of silver curls. "As you can see, I have a fondness for flowers."

"Wait a minute. Let me get this straight." I plant my hands on my hips. "You expect me to believe you're an angel sent from heaven to . . . what?" My mind spins, grasping for logic. Then it lands right back in the hollow. "To protect me? To keep me safe?"

"And to help you clean out the house," she adds cheerfully.

I glance skyward. "You could've just sent me a bodyguard and a housekeeper."

Blossom cackles, a sound that fills the air like music, warming me from the inside out. "I'm here for other reasons too, sugar. But we'll get to those in due time. For now . . ." She steps aside with a flourish, revealing a large orange construction dumpster. "I come bearing gifts."

A smile spreads across my face. "Brilliant! I wish I'd thought of that. Having a guardian angel could come in handy."

"And this is just the beginning, my friend," Blossom says, looping her arm through mine as we enter the house together.

We work straight through lunch, pushing into the late afternoon, clearing out the living room before tackling the dining room. Blossom lifts one end of the heavy pieces of furniture with ease while I struggle to keep up with her. Somehow, we wrestle the sofa, recliner, and several other unsalvageable items to the dumpster.

"I'm done for the day. I couldn't take another step if my life depended on it," I say, collapsing into a rocker on the front porch.

"But look at our progress," Blossom says, sweeping an arm at the now half-full dumpster. "At this rate, we'll be finished by noon tomorrow." She plops down in the rocker beside me, her expression turning serious. "What happened in this house?"

I grunt. "You're the angel. You tell me."

"I don't have all the answers, sugar." She jerks a thumb over her shoulder at the house. "Somebody tore through here like they were hunting for buried treasure but didn't know where to dig."

I laugh despite myself. "That's one way to put it." My smile fades. "I'm hoping it was a random break-in."

"What about the graffiti? *D V* doesn't sound like random hoodlums looking for a thrill. That sounds like somebody marking their territory."

An icy shiver travels my spine. *Marking their territory?* "What could anyone possibly want with a sixty-four-year-old woman?"

"You tell me. What did the police say?"

I shake my head. "I haven't talked to the police. Only Mama's estate attorney. He claims she died from old age. But she was only sixty-four."

Blossom grunts. "Did you pressure him for more information?"

"He was either unable or unwilling to tell me much. He's supposed to be putting me in touch with someone from the sheriff's office, but I haven't heard from them yet." I chew on my lower lip. "The medical examiner would've known if the intruders killed her. Maybe she had a heart attack when she realized she was being robbed."

"Mm-hmm. Maybe," Blossom says, stroking the loose skin on her neck. Her beauty is timeless. I can't tell if she's thirty or fifty.

Blossom heaves her plump body out of the chair. "I don't know about you, but I've worked up quite an appetite. I have a hankering for chicken and dumplings. May I borrow your kitchen?"

I look over at her. "You mean, you're staying overnight?"

Blossom bobs her head, her coils bouncing with the

motion. "Yes, ma'am. I'll stay as long as it takes. If that's okay with you."

After what happened to Mama, I'm not sure how I feel about sleeping in the same house with a stranger. Then again, I enjoy Blossom's company, and I'd rather not be alone, stranger or not.

"Of course. You can sleep in my sister's room."

"Heavens, no. I wouldn't think of putting you out at a time like this. I brought my own accommodations. My Celestial Cruiser." Blossom gestures at a sky-blue mini school bus parked near the dumpster.

I nearly topple over. "Where did that come from? I swear it wasn't there five minutes ago."

Blossom laughs, a cackling sound that warms my heart. "Sure, it was. You just didn't notice," she teases.

Pushing myself out of the rocker, I move to the edge of the porch for a better look. "Your Celestial Cruiser is *tiny*. Surely, there's not enough room for you to sleep in there."

Blossom comes to stand beside her. "You'd be surprised. There's a full-size bed, a toilet and shower combo, and a kitchenette."

I try to picture Blossom maneuvering her large frame in the tiny space, bumping elbows against the walls as she cooks in the kitchenette or squeezes into the shower. Then it hits me —where she's from. That tiny bus is probably bigger and fancier inside than a penthouse suite at The Ritz.

Six

1979

Mama discouraged all leisurely activities. We weren't allowed to play games, didn't own a television, and only listened to classical music and church hymns. Anything that brought pleasure, any source of entertainment, was strictly forbidden.

We were extremely well read. We devoured the classics and, on occasion, were allowed to choose our own novels, although Mama always had the final say. She was well-versed in math and the sciences and made sure we were too. We studied six days a week, with only Sundays off—for worship and chores.

But even with Mama's rigid rules, creativity found a way to sneak in.

I discovered my talent by accident on my eighth birthday, a sweltering June fourteenth. Mellie and I sat cross-legged on a blanket beneath the sprawling oak by the water, dutifully working on our school assignments. But as the afternoon dragged on, restlessness took hold. Bored, I flipped to a clean sheet of notebook paper and let my pencil wander. Without thinking, I began sketching the green heron from the nearby marsh pond. To my amazement, as the lines took shape, the bird seemed to come alive on the page.

When Mama came to check on our progress, I waved the paper excitedly. "Look, Mama! Look what I drew."

She snatched the paper from my hands, barely looking at it before crumpling it into a ball. "Drawing is a senseless waste of time. You're supposed to be focused on your assignments."

Beside me, Mellie stifled a giggle, but Mama's sharp glare found her instantly. "And what is that hideous thing around your neck?"

Mellie's hand flew to the delicate cage of twisted wire cradling a chunk of blue-green sea glass—the treasure she'd found on our beach and carefully strung onto a strip of worn leather.

Mama didn't wait for an answer. With a swift yank, she tore the necklace from Mellie's neck. "Where'd you get this?"

Mellie shot to her feet, reaching for it. "I made it myself! Give it back."

"Meyer women don't wear cheap trinkets. One day, when you're old enough, you'll own the real deal—diamonds, sapphires, emeralds. Until then, you'll do without." Mama dropped the necklace in Mellie's outstretched hand. "You may keep this on your nightstand. Now sit down and get back to work."

Mellie stuffed the necklace in her pocket and sank back onto the blanket.

"Now, girls, I have to leave for work. I'll be gone overnight."

While I cherished the freedom her absence afforded me, I didn't feel safe when she was gone. "But it's my birthday," I protested. "Why do you have to leave us when your work is in the barn?"

"That's only part of my work. My real work is delivering babies for young women in proper families. Soon, you'll begin learning the practice. One day, when you're grown, you'll be a midwife too."

When she spoke about her work, Mama's features always softened. For a fleeting moment, she almost looked pretty.

Mellie wrinkled her nose. "Eww. Gross. I'm not delivering any babies."

Mama's face hardened again. "I beg your pardon. Malone women have been midwives since our family came over on the first boat from England."

Mellie crossed her arms with a huff. "Then let Liddy do it. I'm going to be something else."

Mama stared her down. "You're going to be some lucky man's wife. You'll take care of his home, bear his children, and be the perfect hostess for his guests. But you'll also be a midwife. As the firstborn, it's your birthright—your duty and privilege—to carry on the family practice."

Mama turned her back on us, striding off toward the truck, calling over her shoulder, "Finish your studies and get to your chores. I left some soup for you to reheat in the refrigerator."

Mellie and I sat in silence, watching Mama drive away with the window rolled down and gospel music blaring from the stereo.

Once the dust had cleared, I asked, "Who are the Malone women, Mellie?"

"Women on her side of the family. Her mama, our grandmama, and so on. Marsh Hollow is the Malone family's home."

I knew my mother was an only child and that her parents were both dead. "What about the Meyer family's home? How come we've never met our father's parents—our other grandparents?"

Mellie shrugged. "Maybe they're dead too," she said, gathering her books.

"Where are you going?" I asked, even though I already

knew the answer. Whenever Mama left the farm, Mellie headed straight for the woods.

"None of your business. You stay here and finish your work. I'll be back soon." Mellie got to her feet, stuffing the small notebook she always carried with her in the waistband of her denim shorts.

I watched my sister's figure grow smaller, her back straight and resolute, as she crossed the fields and disappeared into the shadowy entrance to the woods. I counted out loud to sixty—five times—before hurrying after her. I almost always spied on Mellie in the cemetery, watching as she wandered from grave to grave, making seemingly endless notations in her journal. I never got close enough to see the inscriptions on the headstones, and Mellie never left her journal unattended, not even when she was in the bathroom.

I didn't dare sneak into the cemetery alone. I feared the souls of the dead people buried there would suck the life from me like they'd done to my sister. Mellie hadn't been the same since discovering the cemetery. She was different now. Distant. Shadows clung to her in ways they never had before. She used to whisper secrets to me in the dark, but six months ago, she announced she needed her own space and moved across the hall to the guest room. Now, she barely even looked at me. And when she did, her gaze was sharp, edged with something I couldn't name.

From my vantage point behind the trunk of the enormous oak tree, I could barely make out the statue at the rear of the cemetery—cloaked in darkness, standing as if waiting. I wasn't sure if the figure was meant to be a guardian or something far more sinister. Whatever it was, Mellie spent a lot of her time there.

Mellie was usually too preoccupied to notice me, but that day, when a shift of my foot snapped a brittle twig, her head jerked up. "Is someone there? Lydia, is that you?"

My pulse pounded so hard I swore she could hear it. I squeezed my eyes shut and willed myself into stillness, my fingers digging into the rough bark at my back. If I didn't move, if I didn't breathe, maybe she wouldn't see me. Maybe she would go back to whispering to the statue—back to whatever secret world she now belonged to.

"Fine! Do what you want!" she called out. "I can't stop you from coming here. But it's kinda creepy, and I don't want you to be afraid."

For a moment, her voice sounded like the old Mellie, the sister who used to care, who used to watch out for me. But then she turned away, her attention back on whatever she was reading.

I waited until she was focused again before sneaking back to the house.

That night, after brushing my teeth, I crawled into bed with my sister. "How do babies get in their mommy's bellies?"

Mellie sighed like I was the dumbest person alive. "The baby's daddy puts them there. Duh."

A cold fear curled in my stomach. I yanked the covers over my head. "Are you sure about that?" I asked, my voice muffled by the blanket.

"I'm positive," Mellie said. "Read the story about Adam and Eve in your Bible."

"Oh, right. How does the daddy put the baby there?"

"Good grief, Liddy. If you need a lesson in the birds and bees, ask Mama."

"What do the birds and bees have to do with it?"

Mellie let out a huff of irritation. "We live on a farm, Liddy. Why do you think our animals hump each other?"

I thought about that for a minute. "I guess that makes sense. Is our daddy buried in that cemetery?"

"No, dummy. His last name is Meyer, not Malone."

"Oh. Why doesn't Mama ever talk about him?"

"I don't know. Stop asking stupid questions," Mellie snapped, her tone suddenly sharp.

I rolled onto my side. "Fine. Maybe I'll ask Mama."

Mellie said nothing right away. I thought she'd fallen asleep until I heard her shift under the covers.

"Maybe you shouldn't, Liddy. Some things are better left alone," she murmured, her voice barely above a whisper.

A shiver ran down my spine. I wasn't sure if it was her words or the way she said them—like a warning.

I lay awake long after that, staring at the ceiling, wondering why it suddenly felt like there were more secrets in our house than stars in the sky.

Seven

2008

I've never eaten chicken and dumplings before, and I'm blown away by the hearty goodness. The tender, slow-cooked chicken, pillowy dumplings, and rich, creamy broth leave me savoring every bite. The meal is rounded out with moist homemade cornbread and a crisp mixed green salad, drizzled with a bright lemon vinaigrette.

"Blossom, you are a fabulous cook. I don't remember the last time I enjoyed a meal this much, and I worked twenty-two years for two of the best Italian chefs on the East Coast."

Blossom flashes a toothy grin. "Glad you approve. The atmosphere adds a little something extra, don't you think?"

We are seated at the picnic table on the screened porch, where a fresh burst of honeysuckle dances on the breeze.

I prop my elbow on the table, sighing dreamily. "Mm-hmm. Marsh Hollow is lovely this time of year."

"So . . . what're your plans for the house?"

My smile fades. "I'm not sure. I'll probably sell it."

Blossom's emerald eyes widen. "You can't be serious. I figured you'd fix it up with a fresh coat of paint and some new furniture."

I look over at her, brows furrowed. "In case you haven't noticed, this old house needs a lot more than paint and furniture. The repairs alone would cost a small fortune. Unfortunately, I don't have that kind of money. Besides, I have a generous offer from a real estate developer."

Blossom clucks her tongue. "What a shame. I've traveled the world, but I've rarely seen such majestic wildlife."

My gaze drifts over the overgrown fields. Off in the distance, I spot what I think is a bald eagle. "Even if I wanted to stay, there are too many bad memories here."

Blossom drags her cornbread through a puddle of dumpling sauce. "Then why bother coming back? Why not just hire someone to clean it out?"

I hesitate, running my fingertip along the rim of my glass. "In my younger days, I dabbled in art—call it a childhood passion. But when I ran away at sixteen, I left behind my talent. My potential to be an artist."

Blossom cocks an eyebrow. "And now you're hoping to reclaim it?"

"Something like that. I've tried to paint a few times, but the canvas always stays blank. My creativity feels tied to this place. The only wildlife and scenery that have ever inspired me are here, at Marsh Hollow."

"Or what if the house is holding your talent hostage?"

I tilt my head, considering. "That's an interesting way of looking at it. Maybe not the house itself. Maybe the memories."

Blossom wipes her lips with her paper napkin. "I'd like to see your work. Did you keep any of your art from when you were young?"

I shake my head, then pause as I remember the trunk in the attic. "Actually, there may be some things in the attic. I'll go check."

Sliding off the wooden bench, I carry my plate to the kitchen and set it in the sink before heading for the stairs.

Blossom follows close behind. When we get to the top of the stairs, she says, "What's in here?"

I spin around, nerves on heightened alert. "Don't go in there! That's Mama's room!"

Blossom reaches out and touches my arm, grounding me. "Your mama is gone, Lydia. Whatever is in that room won't hurt you."

I wrench my arm free. "The memories can!"

"Then we'll wait for another time to go in there. Obviously, you're not ready." Blossom walks ahead of me down the hall. "Which room is yours?"

"Last one on the right," I say, following behind her into the sunny corner room overlooking the dandelion fields.

"This room holds powerful energy," Blossom says, turning in slow circles, arms outstretched, face tilted toward the ceiling. "Beneath the sorrow, there's a warmth—an unshakable love that still lingers."

"My sister and I shared this room when we were little. There was a lot of love between us then," I say, blinking back unexpected tears.

Without pressing me with questions, Blossom places a reassuring hand on my back, her warm presence offering comfort until the wave of emotion passes.

After a long minute, I inhale a deep breath. "Are we ready to go to the attic?"

"After you," Blossom says with a smile, motioning me to lead the way.

I open the door across the hall, revealing a narrow wooden staircase. "Watch your step, and hold on to the railing," I call over my shoulder to Blossom.

I'm unprepared for the chaos waiting in the attic. Boxes lay torn open, their contents strewn haphazardly across the floorboards. Yellowed papers flutter in the draft from a cracked window, and faded photographs are scattered like fallen leaves. Old trunks, once neatly stacked, have been overturned, their lids hanging open, revealing clothing, books, and shattered keepsakes. The musty air is thick with the scent of dust and neglect, but beneath it lingers something more unsettling—the unmistakable trace of intrusion.

My heart sinks. "I didn't even think to check up here. Why would the intruders have been in our attic?"

Blossom gives me a pointed look. "You tell me."

My shoulders sag. "I guess you were right. They weren't just ransacking the place—they were looking for something specific. But what could my mother possibly have had that would've been of value to anyone?"

"Good question. Since you haven't heard from the sheriff's office, maybe you should try calling them."

"Maybe. But truth be told, my mother's troubles have nothing to do with me. I just want to clean up this house as quickly as possible so I can get back home to Richmond."

Blossom tilts her head. "Are you sure about that? Seems to me this house still has some things to say."

I roll my eyes. "You're being ridiculous. A house can't talk."

"Then what's all that?" She gestures at a stack of boxes labeled in the neat cursive I recognize as my mother's—*linens, china, crystal*.

My brow furrows. "That's odd. Wonder where those came from. I never remember us having guests." I shove one of the boxes aside, frustration bubbling up. "It'll take me forever to sort through all this."

"It doesn't have to be done today, Lydia. This mess isn't going anywhere."

I nod. "True. At least it's out of the way up here, and I

don't have to look at it. If I sell to the developer, he'll bulldoze it. Bye bye mess."

Blossom arches a brow. "Bulldoze it? Your family's home gone in a poof, just like that?" she says, snapping her fingers.

I shrug. "It's not my problem."

Her gaze sweeps the attic, her expression unreadable. "And you're really okay with that?"

"Sure! Why not? I left this place behind a long time ago." But as I turn my back on Blossom, the words ring hollow. The thought of my childhood home reduced to rubble sits like a stone in my gut. Maybe I'm not as ready to let go as I thought.

I find my trunk tucked away in the far corner of the attic, right where I left it. The open lid reveals a jumble of rolled-up paper scraps, yellowed with age, tied with snippets of satin ribbon and lengths of kitchen twine. If anything is missing, I wouldn't know. What could anyone possibly want with a child's art projects?

Choosing a scroll, I untie the pale-blue ribbon and unroll it. Blossom's breath catches at the sight of the egret, its slender neck curved as it feeds in the hollow, framed by yellow-green marsh grass and the soft glow of pink dawn.

"That is stunning, Lydia. An art lover would pay a fortune for it."

I huff a laugh. "Are you kidding me? It's just colored pencils on a scrap of paper."

Blossom shakes her head, her eyes still fixed on the drawing. "But the way you capture it—the detail, the light—it's breathtaking. That's what makes it special."

One by one, we untie the ribbons and unroll the drawings and watercolors—landscapes, birds, quiet moments captured in color and light.

Blossom lingers over a watercolor of the dandelion fields, running a gentle finger along the edge. "God has given you a beautiful gift, Lydia. You must find a way to reclaim it."

"You make it sound so easy." I try to sound indifferent, but the strain in my voice betrays me.

Blossom meets my gaze, her expression steady, knowing. "It doesn't have to be difficult. And I take back what I said earlier. Neither the house nor your memories are holding your talent hostage." She pauses, letting the truth hang between us. "You are."

Blossom insists on bringing some of my artwork downstairs. "As a reminder of what you're capable of," she claims.

I reluctantly agree to let her hang a few in the kitchen to cover up the graffiti.

Afterward, we take steaming mugs of chamomile tea outside to the rockers on the front porch, watching the sunset paint the sky in soft oranges and pinks.

Blossom inhales a deep breath, closing her eyes as she exhales it. "This place is glorious. Once you rediscover your gift, you're never gonna leave."

I rest my head against the back of the rocker, trying to imagine living here—waking up to the sunrise over the creek, watching the tides shift with the seasons. "I don't have a trust fund, Blossom. What would I live on?"

"Your art, of course," she says, a mischievous smirk tugging at her lips.

I snort. "Even if I could sell a few paintings, it would take years for me to build a name for myself."

"Then you find something to tide you over until you strike it big."

I consider the idea. "I guess I could waitress at a local restaurant. That would still give me plenty of time to paint." I shake my head, dismissing it just as quickly. "Forget it. My life is in Richmond."

Blossom angles her body toward me. "Tell me about that life."

"Well . . . I own a nice townhouse, I belong to an Episcopal church, and my son lives there."

Blossom's face lights up, her caramel skin glowing. "A son? How lovely. Do you see him often?"

My smile fades. "Once or twice a month. He's busy with his music career."

"So there's not much tying you to Richmond. If you sold your townhouse, you could use that money to renovate this house."

"No way!" I cut my eyes at her. "I have sweat equity in that townhouse. I raised my son there. I am not a game piece for you to shuffle around."

Blossom rests a hand on my forearm. "No one is playing games with your life, Lydia. I just want you to see you have choices."

"There is only one option, Blossom—fix up this place and sell it. I came here to see if I could reconnect with my creativity. And if that doesn't work out, at least I'll know I gave it an honest try."

My sharp tone makes Blossom shrink back. "I didn't mean to upset you. I get ahead of myself sometimes. I should let my Soul Seekers work through their challenges in their own time."

Guilt twists in my gut. Blossom means no ill will, and she's been an enormous help to me so far.

"Your *Soul Seekers*? Is that what you call the mortals with pathetic lives you're sent to fix?"

"Only you can fix your life, Goldie Girl. I'm just here to offer guidance."

I freeze, goose bumps rising on my bare arms. "Why did you call me that? Because of my hair?"

Blossom brushes a lock off my face. "The color is luscious,

like pure spun gold. But no. I called you that because you have a heart of gold."

"Someone else once called me that," I murmur, my voice barely a whisper.

We sit in comfortable silence for a long moment, soaking in the peaceful evening. Finally, I break the stillness. "How do you suggest I reconnect with my so-called gift?"

"You start by revisiting the past. You've buried painful memories that need to be confronted before you can lay them to rest for good."

The mention of those memories sends a sharp pang through my chest, stealing my breath. "But I thought you said my memories weren't holding me hostage."

"Not the memories themselves," she says gently. "It's the weight you carry from them—the silence, the refusal to speak about what happened. That's what's keeping you prisoner."

"I wouldn't even know where to start," I say, resting my elbow on the chair's arm and burying my face in my hand.

"Why don't we start with the young man who broke your heart?"

My eyes widen. "You mean, Gunner? How did you know about him?"

Sliding down in her chair, Blossom props her feet up on the wicker ottoman. "You can't keep secrets from me. Now start talking."

Eight

1987

On a sweltering June day in a summer that promised to break heat records, I was sketching schools of minnows skimming the still water's surface when the rumble of an outboard motor shattered the silence, pulling me from my reverie.

I looked up, watching the skiff's progress make its way around the bend toward me. As the flat-bottom boat drew closer, the face of the young man at the helm came into view. In my limited experience with men, I'd never seen one so . . . pretty. Or whatever word people used to describe a truly good-looking man. Dark chestnut curls flopped over his forehead, and his pale eyes gleamed like crystal balls in the sunlight. And when he spoke, his voice was as smooth and sweet as honey fresh from the hive.

"Hey there, Golden Girl. Aren't you lonely sitting out here all by yourself? Would you like some company?"

I opened my mouth to speak, but my tongue was tied up in knots.

"I'll take that as a yes." Silencing his engine, he stepped onto the dock and secured his rope around a piling. "What're you working on?" he asked, plopping down beside me, his feet dangling over the side.

"Nothing." I snapped my composition book closed.

"Come on. Let me see. Pretty please," he said, a smile gently playing on his lips as he tugged the book free of my hands.

He opened to the drawing of the minnows and let out a low whistle. "This is great. I'm impressed you captured the sun shimmering off the water with a pencil."

I sat in silence, my cheeks warming, as he flipped through the pages of my notebook. "Are you an artist?" he asked.

"It's just a hobby," I murmured. "But maybe one day."

"Ah . . . a dreamer. I get it. I know what that's like."

When I didn't respond, he asked, "Are you always this quiet? Do you have autism or something?"

I scrunched up my face. "Autism? I don't know what that is?"

He tapped his temple. "You know. Are you mentally challenged?"

"Oh! No! There's nothing wrong with my brain. I'm just not used to talking to strangers. I live on this farm with only my mama and sister."

His eyes widened. "Really? Don't you go to school?"

"Nah. Mama teaches us everything we need to know."

"Whoa. That's insane. I have to say, Golden Girl, that you're the most interesting thing that's happened to me so far this summer."

I giggled nervously. "My name is Lydia."

"And that's a very pretty name, but I prefer Golden Girl—Goldie for short. I'm Gunner, by the way."

I clamp my hand over my mouth to hide my smile.

Gunner tilted his head. "What's so funny?"

"Your name. I've never heard it before. It sounds funny."

He smirked. "I was named after my father, who was named after his father, and all the way back five generations."

"So that makes you the fifth?" I asked.

Gunner rolled his eyes. "Something like that." He extended his hand toward me. "Nice to meet you."

I glanced down at his hand, then back up at him.

"You're supposed to shake hands when you meet someone," he said with a teasing smile, taking my right hand in his and gently squeezing it.

His soft touch sent a wave of warmth through me, leaving me feeling cozy and slightly breathless.

"Oh. I didn't know."

He shook his head, as though bewildered. "Don't you have television?"

"No. Mama says idle minds are the devil's playground, and television is his fancy stage."

"Dang, Goldie. That's really backwards."

When Gunner set his crystal eyes on me, I squirmed, feeling as though he could see straight through to my soul.

"You're the most socially awkward person I've ever met," he said with a grin. "I don't mean that in a bad way. You're a breath of fresh air compared to the other girls I know."

I lowered my gaze, unsure of what to say.

"I'm parched. Could I bother you for something to drink?" Gunner asked.

"Sure! Mama doesn't let us have soda, but I can offer you some lemonade."

Gunner nodded. "Lemonade sounds perfect."

"I'll be right back," I said, scrambling to my feet and dashing up the short dock, across the yard to the house.

As I filled two glasses with ice and lemonade, my mind raced. Mama would beat me senseless if she saw me talking to a boy. Thankfully, she was out of town, delivering the Randolph baby. Before leaving that morning, she warned she might be gone for several nights. It was the mother's first baby, and the birth was breech.

Naturally, Mellie had vanished not long after Mama left. She was likely wandering the woods or combing nearby beaches for sea glass.

When I returned to the dock, I found Gunner studying my drawings. I snatched it back and handed him a glass of lemonade.

"Do you live near here?" I asked, sitting cross-legged on the dock.

Gunner gulped half the glass of lemonade, then leaned back against a piling with a contented sigh. "My parents have a vacation home about a mile away. My father exiled me here for the summer. Apparently, I'm supposed to be figuring out my life."

A puzzled expression crossed my face. "Is there a problem with your life?"

"I just graduated from college in May, and I'm starting a job with a Wall Street brokerage firm in August. Dad's convinced my passion for songwriting will interfere with my career. I'm supposed to spend the summer writing songs, hoping to get it out of my system. As if that's even possible."

"Cool! What type of songs do you write?" I asked, though my exposure to music was limited to the hymns I sang during Mama's Sunday morning prayer services.

"Alternative rock. Think Red Hot Chili Peppers," he said, tugging a silver object from his pocket. He blew into it, producing a high-pitched, whiny sound, then began to sing about a beautiful girl with golden hair who lived in the marsh.

The lyrics flowed like poetry, but I barely noticed them. His voice—smooth yet raw, laced with an emotion that stirred something deep inside me—captivated me completely.

I didn't realize I was crying until he finished.

"I have that effect on most women," he said with a soft chuckle, brushing away my tears with his fingertips.

I grabbed his wrist, pulling his hand away from my face. "I'd like to hear more of your music. Your real music, not made-up songs about me."

"Shall I come back tomorrow? I can bring a picnic lunch and my guitar. I'll serenade you until you beg me to stop."

I burst out laughing. "I don't think that will happen. I could listen to you sing until eternity."

He placed a hand on the back of my neck, pulling me close, and kissed me lightly. The feel of his soft lips on mine sent tingles skimming down my spine, curling my toes. For a moment, the world hushed, with no mama fussing at me to do my homework, no eyes watching my every move. Just this moment—sweet, breathless, and mine.

Nine

2008

"I guess you'll be leaving now that we've finished clearing out the house," I say to Blossom over bowls of hearty tomato soup for lunch the next day.

"You can't get rid of me that easy. My work here has just begun." She glances at her watch. "We have the whole afternoon to kill. There's a secondhand home furnishings store in Colton. We could make the trip into town, see if they have some things to replace the items you lost."

My brow shoots up. "How do you know about the secondhand shop?"

"Google," Blossom says with a chuckle.

I stare at her, aghast. "But we don't have internet service out here."

Blossom waves a hand at her mini bus. "I have a connection in my mobile Command Center."

I laugh. "I'm sure you do. One of everything else too."

Blossom mops up the rest of her soup with a chunk of French bread. "So, about that trip to town? I'll even treat you to an ice cream," she says in a tempting tone.

I lower my gaze, staring into my empty bowl. "I don't

think so. My gut tells me to pack up my belongings and head for the hills."

Blossom lets out an exasperated huff. "Well, this is one time I'd advise you not to trust your gut."

"What's the point of buying furniture if I'm just going to sell the house to the developer?"

Blossom dropped her spoon into her bowl with a clang. "Is that decision final?"

I shrug. "I've been toying with the idea since I got here. I told you that."

"You're being stubborn, Goldie Girl," Blossom shoots back. "If you don't wanna go shopping for furniture, then get out your art supplies and paint yourself a picture."

Telling Blossom about Gunner had the opposite effect. Instead of feeling more inspired to create, my talent seems unreachable—trapped in the past, forever lost. But I've come all this way. If I don't at least try while I'm here, I'll always wonder what might have been.

"Maybe I will," I say, standing abruptly. I drop my bowl off in the kitchen and continue toward the stairs, pausing in the living room to contemplate the empty space. The house feels lighter now. I imagine a fresh taupe-colored paint on the walls, a linen-covered sofa in a similar shade, a sisal rug underfoot, and pillows in hues of blue and green—the colors of the Chesapeake Bay.

Oh well. I'll leave the decorating to the next owner. Except there won't be a next owner if I sell Marsh Hollow to the developer. At least, not in this house. He'll likely divide the property into eight or ten larger lots and build sprawling vacation homes for families with young children or retirees.

The thought disheartens me, though I'm not sure why. Will I actually miss this house? But what about all the terrible memories that still reside here?

Ugh. I need off this emotional roller coaster. One minute

I'm ready to sell, the next I'm imagining living out my days here. I shake my head, reminding myself that I don't have the means to renovate or maintain this place. Mama had let it go so far downhill, I'd need mountain climber gear to get it back where it once was.

Grabbing pen and sketch pad from my room, I head down to dock for the first time since my return. When I get there, I'm surprised to find that many of the cedar planks are new. Why would Mama repair the dock—when she didn't own a boat—but not the brick front steps?

Sitting down on the fresh wood, I lean against a piling, tilting my face skyward to the warm sun. My mind drifts back twenty-two years. Gunner is beside me with his guitar in hand, serenading me with his smooth voice while I sketch.

Memories flood me, drawing me back to the sultry days of my sweet-sixteen summer, pressing against me like an unrelenting wave. They're as vivid as if they happened yesterday, and I desperately need to let them out.

Opening my eyes, I sit up straight, tucking my legs to my chest. Flipping open my sketch pad, I hover the pen over the blank page. But instead of sketching, I begin to write. My words spill onto the page in vivid detail—the sulfuric scent of the marsh, the honking of geese in the distance, and the tickle of a light breeze against my skin.

The rumble of an outboard motor pulls me from my words. Still lost in the past, I look up from my sketchbook, half-expecting to see Gunner.

"Ahoy there!" calls the sandy-haired man behind the steering wheel. "Permission to tie up at your dock?"

I chuckle. "Permission granted," I say, offering a playful salute.

As he secures the boat, I take him in. He looks to be about my age, his gray T-shirt stretches over broad shoulders, and his tanned legs are visible beneath well-worn khaki work shorts.

He has a likable face—handsome in an easy, unassuming way rather than striking—and eyes the color of slate.

"I'm Sam Whitaker. I live across the creek," he says, aiming a thumb over his shoulder. "I saw the construction dumpster and thought I'd offer my services. I'm a handyman. Mostly small projects, though I've built entire houses before. I did a few odd jobs for Aurelia. I'm sorry about her passing. Are you family?"

I'm not used to hearing Mama referred to by her given name. *Aurelia.* The name belongs to someone timeless and charming—not a woman as cold as my mother. "I'm her daughter."

Curiosity flickers across his face. "Oh. I didn't realize she had a daughter."

I hold up two fingers. "I'm the youngest."

"Nice to meet you," he says, closing the distance between us with an extended hand.

Closing my sketchbook, I stand to face him, accepting the handshake. "Nice to meet you too, Sam. I'm Lydia Meyer. What sort of jobs do you do? Is this your handiwork?" I ask, gesturing at the new planks on the dock.

Sam laughs. "It is. Aurelia was worried about someone falling through the rotten old boards, but I never could convince her to let me repair the crumbling brick steps at her front door."

"Ha! I was just wondering about that."

He shakes his head in bewilderment. "I even offered to do the labor for free. She claimed she couldn't afford the brick. As a favor to Aurelia, I can give you the same rate."

"I appreciate your kind offer, but I'm thinking of selling the property to a developer."

Sam's smile fades, his blue-gray eyes darkening. "A *developer*? That would be unfortunate. Those land sharks will tear down every single tree and replace them with cookie-cutter houses in a sterile country club setting. The new residents will be so distracted by their golf games, pool parties, and tennis matches that they'll never enjoy the beauty of the world around them."

I swallow past the unexpected lump in my throat. "That's not exactly what I had in mind. I'm thinking larger lots and fewer homes."

Sam shakes his head. "Once you sell to a developer, he can do whatever he wants with it."

"That's true," I concede, glancing up at the house. "But I don't have the money for repairs, let alone ongoing maintenance."

Sam follows my gaze. "The house isn't in as bad a shape as you might think. It needs a facelift, sure. But many of the repairs you could handle yourself."

I'm curious just how friendly he and Mama were. I can't imagine her inviting him in for afternoon tea. Does he even know about the vandalism? "Have you ever been in the house?"

"Once. To fix a broken kitchen faucet. But the outside is mostly sound. The shutters need some work, and the gutters need replacing—manageable tasks that aren't too costly. Believe it or not, the house was built like a fortress. They don't make 'em like that anymore." Sam nods at the house. "Shall we take a look?"

I shrug. "I guess."

We walk up the dock in silence, stopping in the yard to take in the house.

"You can address drafts by sealing windows and doors," Sam explains. "That's something you can do yourself. It'll improve energy efficiency, cutting down on your electric bill."

"I appreciate your vote of confidence, Sam, but I wouldn't even know where to start."

"I'd be happy to help you," he says with a genuine smile that makes me feel warm all over.

Blossom emerges from the house, waving at us from the porch. We shorten the distance to her, and I introduce them.

"Sam's a handyman, Blossom. He did some minor repairs for Mama."

"Very nice to meet you, Sam," Blossom says, clapping him on the shoulder.

A box truck pulls up to the house. "Who's that?" I ask. "I'm not expecting a delivery."

"I made a quick trip to that secondhand furniture store I mentioned," Blossom says with a devilish grin. "They had exactly what you're looking for. I even got you a good deal on a barely used, wide-screen TV."

Two men in gray uniforms begin unloading furniture— pieces identical to what I'd imagined earlier.

"Put everything in the center of the living room and cover it with blankets," Blossom instructs them.

"We'll paint before we arrange the furniture," Blossom informs us. "I picked up some paint while I was out. I chose a pretty color called pale oak, a soft shade of taupe with just a hint of pink. We can knock out the painting in a day."

Sam's hand shoots up. "Count me in!"

I stare at him, dumbfounded. "Why would you help us when you don't even know me?"

He grins. "Because I'm a sucker for a fixer-upper, and this house has good bones. Besides, I'm not working on anything pressing at the moment. I'm driving myself crazy with nothing to do."

"You're kind, Sam, but I don't feel right about asking a complete stranger to paint my house."

Blossom jabs an elbow into my ribs. "Don't look a gift horse in the mouth," she mutters.

Sam laughs. "Blossom has a point. While I'm here, I can

go over the house with a fine-tooth comb and make a list of what needs immediate attention."

I consider his offer. Where's the harm in finding out the extent of the required repairs? "Why not? We'll start first thing in the morning."

"Excellent. I'll be here around eight," Sam says, backing away a few steps before turning toward the dock.

"He seems like a nice man," Blossom says.

I know what she's thinking, but I refuse to look at her. "I guess," I say, my eyes on Sam's boat as it pulls away.

"Did you have success?" she asks, eyeing my sketchbook.

"I'll let you decide." I tear out the written pages and hand them to Blossom.

Blossom glances down at my tidy print covering the pages. "What's this?"

"You wanted to know more about Gunner. I find it easier to write about my feelings than talk about them."

Blossom presses the pages to her chest, her smile warm and full of understanding. "Thank you for trusting me with your words. It doesn't matter how they come out—only that you let them leave your heart."

Ten

1987

I spent every waking hour with Gunner while Mama was away. Each morning, he arrived shortly after breakfast and stayed until late afternoon. We explored the marshes and fields, taking long, meandering boat rides along the banks of the Chesapeake Bay.

I introduced him to my world—the wild tangle of spartina grass, the way the light played on the water at dusk, the hidden hollow where the egrets nested.

He shared stories of his college years at the University of Virginia. Fraternity parties, football games, late-night drives down the Blue Ridge Parkway with the windows down and music blasting—his world sounded as distant from mine as the moon. He was fascinated by my life, too, the way I had been raised apart from the noise of the world.

We made a hideaway on the narrow beach in the hollow, where he strummed his guitar and wrote songs while I sketched and painted. His voice wove around me like a spell, smooth as river stones, raw with something I didn't fully understand.

We swam in the inlet, taking breaks from the sweltering sun, stealing moments that felt too perfect to last. With each passing day, I clung harder to the illusion that summer would stretch on forever, that we could exist in this untouched world, just the two of us, without time or consequence.

But I never forgot that Mama could return at any minute. On the afternoon of our third day together, I warned him yet again. "Mama has never been gone this long. She should be back any minute. If you hear the crunch of tires on the gravel driveway, you need to leave. Fast!"

We were stretched out on a blanket on the beach, our bodies pressed together, skin still glistening from our swim.

Gunner twirled a damp lock of my hair around his finger. "Geez, Goldie. Relax. I'm not afraid of your mama."

I sat up straight. "You should be. She's mean. I've seen her break a chicken's neck with her bare hands."

He chuckled. "So? Isn't that what farm women do?"

"You don't understand," I said, near tears. "She's liable to throttle you with those same bare hands."

Gunner sat up, his teasing tone now gone. He cupped my chin, forcing me to look at him. "Hey! Hey! Calm down. I promise I won't cause any trouble for you. The second I hear tires on the gravel, I'm gone. She'll never know I was here."

I swallowed hard and nodded. "Okay," I said, taking several deep breaths to steady my nerves.

"And if she comes home during the night," he said, tucking a loose strand of hair behind my ear, "you'll tie a white ribbon around the dock piling like we talked about."

"Right. So you'll know to meet me here in the morning."

"I don't like to see you so upset, Goldie. Whenever you talk about your mama, sadness fills those beautiful eyes, and your face hardens into stone. Now lighten up and let me see that smile again." He kissed and licked my cheeks and jaw until I fell back on the blanket in a fit of giggles.

Our kisses had grown more urgent, and at night, when I lay alone in my darkened room, my thoughts drifted to him, imagining his touch on the places I barely understood—those sweet spots that made my heart race and my cheeks burn.

He fingered the strap of my swimsuit, a one-piece hand-me-down from Mellie. "Why do you wear this frumpy old thing? You'd look great in a bikini."

"Ha. Mama would never allow me to wear a bikini, even if we could afford it. We're not rich like you, Gunner."

"And neither are we, although my father makes a decent living as an attorney. But one day I *will* be wealthy, when I strike it big as a songwriter and music producer."

I admired him for his confidence and envied him for having the freedom to be whoever he wanted to be. "So you've decided to give up your job on Wall Street?"

"No, and I don't think I can. The best thing for me to do is keep writing songs on the side. The right opportunity will eventually come along." Gunner rolled onto his back with his hands behind his head. "I haven't told anyone this, but I've submitted my music to a producer in Los Angeles. I'm waiting to hear back."

My eyes grew wide. "*Los Angeles?* As in California."

He looked over at me as though I'd lost my mind. "There's only one Los Angeles, as far as I know."

"But that's halfway around the world," I said, fear gripping my chest. If he moved so far away, I'd never see him again.

"That's the idea. The farther away from my dad, the better. Besides, it's not halfway around the world. Didn't your mama teach you geography?"

I gave him a playful shove. "Of course. I was exaggerating."

"Are you sure? I can't always tell with you."

"Yes, I'm sure. Los Angeles is in California, which is located on the Pacific Coast. Los Angeles is the largest city with 3.8 million people. Next largest is San Diego, followed by

San Jose, San Francisco, and Fresno. California has the largest economy in the US and the eighth largest in the world. The top university is—"

Gunner clamped a hand over my mouth. "Stop! Please! I get it."

I couldn't read his expression, couldn't tell whether he was teasing or mad. I pried his hand away. "Why are you being so mean?"

"I'm not. I just think it's so bizarre the way she's raising you. You can recite the encyclopedia, but you don't know how to make casual conversation or use a telephone or shop for groceries. How does she expect you to survive when you leave Marsh Hollow?"

"She doesn't," I said, letting the implication hang in the air between us.

"I gotta go. This is starting to be a drag," he muttered, gathering his things and getting to his feet.

My heart raced as I followed him to the dock. "Will I see you tomorrow?"

He shrugged. "I'm not sure. Maybe." He dropped his things into the boat and untied the line.

"If you—"

His hand shot out. "Don't say it. I know to look for the white ribbon."

I watched in silence as his boat sped away, the rumble of the outboard motor fading into the distance. When he was gone, I returned to our camp, collapsed face down on the blanket, and sobbed until my whole body ached. I'd never known this kind of pain—the hollow ache, the unbearable finality of goodbye. The thought of never seeing Gunner again made my chest constrict, as if the very air had been stolen from my lungs.

Dragging myself to my knees, I tilted my face heavenward

and whispered my plea. "Please, God, give me another chance with him. I won't blow it this time, I promise. I'll show him I can be normal—that I'm not the freak he thinks I am. And please, dear Lord, make Mama stay away just one more day."

That night, over tomato and mayonnaise sandwiches for dinner, I asked my sister if she was worried about Mama. "I thought she would've come home by now."

Mellie's brow shot up. "Worried? I'm thrilled. If we're lucky, she got killed in a car accident."

My jaw hit the counter. "Mellie! Don't say such things! God will strike *you* dead."

"I'd rather be dead than live with her one more day," Mellie muttered, stuffing the last bite of sandwich into her mouth.

"I never see you anymore. What have you been doing all this time?" I tried to keep my tone casual, but what I really wanted to know was whether Mellie suspected anything—if she had the faintest idea a boy had been coming to see me.

"Collecting sea glass and making jewelry. Wanna see?" Mellie's smile transformed her face into that of a stunning young woman I barely recognized. It had been years since I'd seen that smile—or the twinkle in her mesmerizing hazel eyes. Even though we lived together, saw each other every single day, Mellie had somehow become a total stranger to me.

"Sure! I'd love to see." I hopped off the stool and followed Mellie up the stairs to her room.

She retrieved an old boot box from the top shelf of her closet and sat down with it on the bed, patting the space beside her. "You can't tell anyone, especially Mama."

I dragged an *X* over my heart. "Promise."

When Mellie removed the lid, chunks of sea glass in every shape, size, and color glimmered inside. She'd used paper clips, twist ties, and kitchen twine to fashion some pieces into necklaces, bracelets, and earrings. Sitting this close, I noticed angry-looking holes in her ears. In Mama's absence, she had pierced them herself.

Mellie rummaged through the box. "This is my favorite," she said, pulling out a thick strip of leather, covered in sea glass fragments, all the same shade of blue-green.

I sucked in a sharp breath. "That's beautiful, Mellie. You're really talented. What will you do with all this?" I took the box from her and ran my finger over the smooth edges of the glass.

Mellie snatched the box back and slammed the lid shut. "This is my ticket out of this godforsaken place."

My stomach flipped. "What do you mean?"

"What do you think I mean?" Mellie returned the box to the closet, closed the door, and leaned against it. "When the time comes, I'm going to New York. I'll get a job working for a jeweler. Then, one day, I'm going to design my own jewelry. I'll be famous and I'll be free. And no one will ever again tell me what to do."

My heart raced. My sister planned to leave me behind. "But what about Mama?"

Mellie snorted. "What about her? I'll be eighteen in a few weeks. Once I'm of age, she can't stop me."

I hesitated, unsure how to respond. I didn't want Mellie to think I was uncool. Especially after Gunner had called me a *drag*. "You could leave now. Take Mama's spare cash out of the coffee can."

"There's not enough in there for a bus ticket. But I wouldn't take it anyway. I want nothing from her. I'm doing this on my own. I'll wait for the right opportunity. One is coming my way. I feel it in my bones." A shiver ran through her.

"What about me?" I asked, no longer trying to hide my desperation.

Mellie's expression didn't soften. "What about you? You're on your own, Liddy. Get out while you can. We were born into this twisted family, and no one is coming to save us."

Eleven

2008

Blossom, Sam, and I work diligently through the morning and early afternoon, painting the living room and rearranging the new furniture. The transformation is remarkable. This once dingy room, now bright and inviting, stuns me. While Sam sets up the wide-screen television on the rustic console table, Blossom and I scrub decades' worth of grime off the windows, letting abundant sunlight cast a warm glow over the room.

Afterward, Sam steps outside to calculate the number of bricks needed to repair the front steps while Blossom and I prepare a picnic lunch.

"Sam is sweet on you, you know?" Blossom says in a knowing voice as she hands me a platter of crispy fried chicken.

I roll my eyes. "Please! He's just being neighborly."

"Mm-hmm. Time will tell." Blossom winks at me. "Keep your mind and heart open to the possibility of romance."

Since Gunner, I've only been on a few blind dates and wouldn't recognize romantic attraction if it bit me in the fanny. Still, I admit I enjoy Sam's company. His easygoing, nonjudgmental nature puts me at ease. And when he tells a funny story, a dimple appears in the corner of his mouth and his blue-gray eyes shimmer like moonlight on water.

We've only just sat down at the table on the back porch when Blossom is on her feet again. "I just remembered—I have an important call in a few minutes. The cell service is better over near my bus. Y'all eat without me."

I smile to myself. She's using the call as an excuse to give me time alone with Sam. But I'm unprepared for the awkward silence that follows. Gunner had been right all those years ago —Mama did me no favors. I've never been good at making casual conversation.

"Have you always wanted to be a handyman?" I blurt out, my face warming at how ridiculous my question sounds. Who dreams of being a handyman?

Sam chuckles, easing the tension. "Actually, yeah. Well, sort of. My father owned a chain of hardware stores in Richmond, and I grew up helping him behind the counter. But after I lost my wife, I sold the chain."

My face falls. "Oh gosh. I'm sorry. What happened to your wife?"

The pain that flashes across his face is so raw I immediately regret asking. "You don't have to answer that. It's none of my business."

His eyes darken like an approaching storm. "It's okay. It's just not easy to talk about." He exhales, then says slowly, "She was killed during a home invasion."

I gasp, my hand flying to my mouth, and immediately think of Mama. Is that what happened here? Was the medical examiner wrong? Then it dawns on me—maybe a violent gang lives nearby. Maybe the same thugs who killed his wife killed Mama. "I'm so sorry, Sam. That's awful. Were you living here at the time?"

"No. In Richmond. It happened on Christmas Eve, ten years ago." A faraway look falls over his face. "A strand of lights had gone out on the Christmas tree, and we were expecting my in-laws for dinner. I ran to the hardware store to pick up more lights. When I came home . . ." His voice falters. "I found her bleeding out on the kitchen floor."

I instinctively reach for his hand—a small gesture, but one that feels right. "How tragic. Do you have any children?"

He shakes his head, his chin dropping to his chest. "She was pregnant with our first child."

"That's the worst thing I've ever heard. I can't imagine how difficult that was for you." I wish I were Blossom right now. She would know exactly what to say.

Sam lifts his chin, giving me an apologetic smile. "I'm sorry for going dark on you. I rarely talk about my wife."

"I'm glad you felt comfortable telling me."

He squeezes my hand, then releases it and reaches for a chicken leg. "What about you? Have you ever been married?"

"No, but I have a grown son. We'll save the story of his father for another day." She bites into a deviled egg. "Now, onto happier subjects. How many bricks will it take to fix the steps?"

He laughs. "No more than a pallet, which is five hundred bricks. Does this mean you're ready to move forward with the project?"

"I'm not sure. I'm terrified someone will hurt themselves on the steps. But I hate to spend the money if I'm—"

Sam cuts me off. "Thinking of selling. To a developer." He pauses, then adds, "Have you considered putting Marsh Hollow on the market? Don't get me wrong—I'd love for you to stay, to be my neighbor. But if you sell, a nice retired couple would be a lot better than a developer."

"I would only get a fraction of what it's worth."

"But you'd be preserving the integrity of the land." He looks at me over the top of his chicken leg. "After lunch, let's walk through the house together. We'll figure out which repairs are urgent, and I'll give you a package price. You'll need to make those improvements before you list it, but you'll get your money back when it sells."

I smile softly. "Okay. I don't see why not."

It feels like a windfall, no matter which path I take. I never expected to inherit anything from Mama. And Sam's right—I'd hate to see the trees torn down, the fields paved over, and the marsh. Would they turn my hollow into a marina?

While I clean up after lunch, Sam moves around the kitchen, jotting down notes as he points out various issues. He reports that—aside from the back-right burner on the stove being out—the appliances are in working order despite their age. The sink pipes need replacing, and the electrical panel tucked inside the pantry will need to be upgraded to meet current safety standards.

As we continue through the downstairs, we discuss modernizing the dining room with more comfortable seating and a new chandelier.

"This is a quaint little nook," Sam says about the small alcove off the living room. Running his hand across the cypress paneling, he adds, "A good cleaning would bring the wood back."

"I was thinking of putting a small desk with a computer by the window."

Sam nudges me playfully with his elbow. "So you *are* considering staying at Marsh Hollow?"

Through the window, I look out over the dandelion fields, envisioning two little girls picking strawberries on a day very much like today. "I didn't mean me. I meant whoever buys the house if I don't sell it to a developer."

"Who will bulldoze this charming house, along with all the memories from your childhood."

I turn toward him, meeting his gaze. "That's exactly the point, Sam."

A long moment passes as my words sink in. "Oh. I'm sorry. I didn't realize. And here I've been pressuring you to stay somewhere that causes you pain."

"Actually, you've been helping me see the house from a different perspective—the potential it has to be someone else's happy home."

He gives me a curious look, head askew. "But not yours?"

I massage my temples. "I don't know. Maybe. I'm confused. I have a lot to sort out."

He squeezes my shoulder. "Don't be so hard on yourself. You'll get there. Being on the water will help. The fresh air, the quiet, the scenery—it's why I moved down here." He takes the notepad from me. "We can stop here for today if it's too much."

I snatch it back. "No! Let's finish. I want to know what the cost of the basic improvements will be."

Sam smiles softly, his eyes full of warmth. "If you're sure. But stop me anytime if it becomes too much."

"I will. Let's go to the second floor," I say, leading him across the living room and up the stairs.

I'm passing my mother's closed door when Sam asks, "What's in here?"

"Don't go in there!" I bark. But it's too late. Sam has already opened the door.

From the hallway, I can see the room has been emptied. The only remaining signs of Mama are the four-poster bed, putrid green carpeting, and the wallpaper covered in yellow rose blossoms.

"Wow," Sam says, stepping inside. "Look at this natural light."

I'm paralyzed with fear, expecting to hear voices from the past, the voices I dreaded as a child. The ones that slithered through the walls late at night, whispering in the dark. Mama's voice, brittle and sharp, would rise and fall in frantic conversation, answering someone only she could hear. There was one name she spoke most often.

Everett. Who was Everett?

I squeeze my eyes shut, forcing the memory back into the shadows where it belongs. That was a long time ago. Mama's gone. Her madness buried with her.

And yet, as I step over the threshold, a shiver skates down my spine.

Because for one terrible second, I swear I hear her.

Sam's hand lands on my shoulder, grounding me. "Lydia, are you okay? You're white as a sheet."

I shake off the eerie feeling, inhaling deeply. "Sorry. Yes, I'm fine." Squaring my shoulders, I cross the threshold.

The room occupies the west wing of the house. Mama had kept the heavy gold velvet drapes closed much of the time. But now, with the draperies gone, sunlight floods in through the double-hung windows that line three of the walls.

I run my fingers over the peeling wallpaper. "This was Mama's room. The door was closed when I arrived, and I've been avoiding it ever since."

Sam opens two doors—one leading to the outdated bathroom and the other a closet, stacked full of cardboard boxes, which I assume contain mama's clothes.

"This would make a great master suite for you," Sam says.

I shake my head. "No way! Even if we stripped the wallpaper and ripped out the carpet, I don't think I could ever sleep in here. Too many ghosts."

"It's a shame to waste this space. And this view." Sam tries to open a window, but it's painted shut. "I've noticed you carrying around a sketch pad. Why not turn it into a studio?"

Excitement flickers in my chest as I picture an easel by the window and shelves neatly lined with my supplies. "I'd have to call in a priest to exorcise Mama's ghost first."

Sam laughs awkwardly, as though trying to decide if I'm

joking. Letting it pass, he kneels and peels back a corner of the carpet. "There are hardwood floors under here." He pulls the carpet back farther. "And they appear to be in excellent condition."

"That's good for the next owner," I said deadpan.

"Which might be you." He strokes his chin as he continues to survey the space. "How do you feel about surprises?"

I hesitate. "I like surprises, I guess. I honestly haven't had many. Why?"

A slow smile creeps across his face. "I have an idea for fixing up the room. I'd like to surprise you."

"That's too much, Sam. I can't ask you to do that. Don't you have any paying clients?"

Sam chuckles. "I do, actually. I'll be starting extensive renovations on an old farmhouse soon. I'm waiting for the architect to send me the final drawings so I can apply for the building permits. But that's still a week away, and I need something to keep me busy now."

I exhale a heavy sigh. "Finish your inspection and give me your preliminary numbers. Then I'll decide how to proceed."

"Fair enough," he says, scribbling notes on his pad.

After a brief tour of the upstairs, Sam retreats to the front porch to complete his estimate while I go to the kitchen for lemonade. When he presents his proposal, my brow furrows. His numbers are much lower than I expected. Studying them more closely, I realize he's only charging me for the cost of the materials.

"I'm not a charity case, Sam. I can't ask you to donate your valuable time for free." I shove the proposal at him, but he refuses to take it.

"I won't be doing all the work myself. I'm counting on you to help me. Blossom too, if she'll be around for a while."

"I'm not sure how long she's staying." I fold the paper and

drop it in my lap. "If not for charity, why are you doing this when we barely know each other?"

"I felt a connection between us when we first met. After spending the day together, I understand why. We are kindred spirits, troubled souls. I don't know how you feel about God, but I think maybe divine intervention brought us together."

Troubled souls? Does Blossom have something to do with this divine intervention? But maybe Sam is right. Maybe we are kindred spirits, both of us trying to rebuild something we lost.

I rest my head on the back of the chair. "Let's start with the brick steps and go from there."

"Deal." A smirk tugs at his lips. "Although it will take a few days to get the bricks delivered. "In the meantime, I'll start on your surprise."

I roll my head on the back of the chair to look at him. "You won't take no for an answer, will you?"

Sam shakes his head. "Nope."

"Just make sure whatever you do appeals to potential buyers."

"Oh, it will. Although I have every intention of convincing you not to sell."

I'm too tired to argue. But I admit, the thought of having him hanging around the house for the next few days sends a little thrill through me.

He glances at his watch. "I should get going. I have some chores to tend to at home."

He rises slowly and I walk with him to the edge of the porch.

"I don't know how to thank you, Sam."

"Your friendship is thanks enough." He winks at me as he steps off the porch.

I'm watching Sam stroll across the yard to the dock when a voice startles me.

"Your eyes are twinklin' like a Christmas tree."

I spin around. "Geez, Blossom! You scared me! Don't sneak up on me like that."

Blossom grins, her gaze following Sam's boat as he speeds across the creek. "He's such a nice man."

"Yes, he is. But you knew that when you brought us together."

Blossom huffs. "If only I had that kind of power."

I cross my arms. "If you have the power to make furniture disappear, you surely have the power to match make."

Blossom plants a hand on her hip. "Now hold on—what furniture are you accusing me of vanishing?"

"Mama's. Her furniture, the draperies—everything's gone. Just the wallpaper's still up, and a few boxes shoved in the closet. Probably her clothes."

Her hands shoot up. "I promise you, Goldie, I had nothing to do with that. You asked me not to go in your mama's room, and I didn't. I will always respect your wishes."

"Who on earth took them then?" I shrug. "Know what? I don't really care. Whoever it was did me a favor. I wish they'd taken the boxes too. I dread going through her things."

"I bet it won't be as bad as you think." Blossom tilts her head, a playful spark in her eyes. "Have you written anymore of your story? I'm dying to know what happens with Gunner."

"I haven't had time today." I glance up at the sky. "But since I still have plenty of daylight left, I'll go work on it now. I should have something for you to read before you go to bed."

Blossom rubs her hands together. "I can hardly wait."

I grab my sketchbook from inside and head down to the dock. A strange urgency grips me, as if finishing the story will help me let go of the past and clear the way for a fresh start. I'm at a crossroads. No matter what, I'll have to find a job— whether I go back to Richmond or stay here. And aside from my son, who I rarely see anyway, there's nothing meaningful tying me to Richmond. The thought of living full-time at Marsh Hollow stirs something deep inside me. The wildlife, the serenity, the beauty of the land—it's good for the soul.

If only I could untangle the beauty of this place from the burden of the past.

Twelve

1987

Mama's return from delivering the Randolph baby put a major cramp in my love life. The long, carefree hours I'd spent with Gunner over the previous few days were reduced to stolen moments in our hidden hollow. But the secrecy of our fleeting time together heightened the urgency of our attraction. I knew being with a man who wasn't my husband was a sin, but when Gunner unbuttoned my blouse and slipped his fingers inside my bra, I didn't stop him. And when he tugged my shorts down and touched my most intimate places, I gasped with desire. I couldn't stop myself if I wanted to. Nor could I stop him.

On the fourth of July, a week after Mama's return, I sneaked out of the house after dark to meet Gunner in the hollow. Fireworks burst across the sky over the bay as I gave myself to him, surrendering beneath a cascade of glittering color. Our first time was rushed and painful, leaving me bewildered. What was all the fuss about? But the next time, Gunner was patient—gentle and attentive—helping me feel things I didn't even know were possible.

"Should we be using protection?" I asked as I lay in his arms afterward. "Mama would kill me if I got pregnant."

"Don't worry. I've got you covered—the tried-and-true withdrawal method works like a charm every time."

His answer seemed reasonable, and I didn't know enough about sex to question him.

At the end of July, Mama announced she was leaving for another extended trip. "I could be gone a while this time. The Waller twins are expecting twins within a week of each other. If I'm driving all the way to Blacksburg, I might as well stay and see both deliveries through."

I kept a straight face as I wished my mother safe travels, but inside, I was buoyant, celebrating my good fortune. I would have a whole glorious week alone with Gunner.

On the second day of Mama's absence, a storm system set in. My sister had disappeared to one of her haunts. So when Gunner arrived that afternoon, I invited him upstairs to my bedroom. Even with Mama out of town, I knew better than to do anything inappropriate. We lay curled up on my bed, fully clothed, talking about his future—as always—when a sharp knock shattered the moment.

"Lydia! Open up! Is someone in there with you?"

Panic rooted me in place as I locked eyes with Gunner. "My sister," I mouthed.

Gunner pressed his lips together, fighting back laughter.

Pressing my hand to his mouth, I called out, "Of course not, Mellie. Who would I have in my room? I'm just talking to myself again."

We remained perfectly still, barely daring to breathe, until we heard Mellie's footsteps retreating down the stairs.

"Do you think she believed you?" Gunner whispered.

"Of course. Who would I even sneak in?" I whispered, but doubt gnawed at me. Did she believe me?

"Still. I should leave. I don't want to get you in trouble."

He stood and tiptoed to the window. "I can crawl across the porch roof and shimmy down that tree if you think it's safer. But it's still pouring rain, and I might slip and fall."

I went to stand beside him at the window. "No way! You could break your leg—or your back. Mellie's probably gone by now anyway. We'll sneak you out the front door."

Taking him by the hand, I led him out of my room and down the stairs. At the bottom, I froze. Mellie was waiting.

She sat stiffly on the sofa, her posture unnaturally rigid, like she was balancing a book on her head the way Mama had taught us. Her gaze alternated between Gunner and me, and though her expression was unreadable, a sly smile tugged at the corner of her mouth.

She jumped up. "I knew it! You *did* have someone in your room. A boy!" Her golden eyes swept over him, appraising him. "A very cute one, I might add."

Gunner's pale eyes widened in surprise, clearly liking what he saw as he took in my beautiful sister. "I'm sorry if we upset you," he said. "We were just talking. I swear."

My heart pounded against my ribs. "Mellie, please don't tell Mama," I pleaded, my voice trembling.

Mellie's expression hardened in an instant. Her gaze turned sharp, calculating. Her arm shot out, finger pointed toward the stairs. "Go to your room, Liddy! We'll discuss this later—in private."

"But—" I protested.

Her tone was like iron. "Now, Liddy! Or I *will* tell Mama."

Tears burned my throat as I darted up the stairs. But I didn't go to my room. I pressed my back against the wall at the top, straining to hear their hushed conversation, but their voices were too low, the words too muffled to make out. Then the front door clicked shut.

I hurried to my bedroom window just in time to see them

running hand in hand through the driving rain toward the dock.

I stayed at the window long after the rain stopped. Watching. Waiting. Praying.

But Mellie never returned home.

The next morning, at first light, I tore through the house looking for her. I checked her room first. Her bed hadn't been slept in.

Panic rose in my throat. No. No, no, no.

I searched the entire property—the barn, the woods, even the cemetery—but Mellie was nowhere to be found.

She left me.

By lunchtime, I was frantic. And when Mellie finally walked through the front door, I saw red. I attacked her, fists flying, tears streaming down my face. "You can't have him! He's mine! You stole him from me!"

Mellie gasped and stumbled backward, shielding herself. But then, her hand found the fireplace poker. She held it out between us like a weapon, keeping me at bay. "He is not yours, Liddy. He is very much his own person. And what he needs right now is guidance, which you have clearly failed to give him."

My breath hitched. Guidance? What did that even mean?

Tucking the poker under her arm, she dashed up the stairs.

I chased her, my pulse pounding, and stopped in her bedroom doorway as she yanked open her closet and started shoving clothes into a trash bag.

"What're you doing?" My voice was barely above a whisper.

Mellie didn't look at me. "I'm leaving this awful place."

My heart dropped to my stomach. "What?"

She tossed the trash bag over her shoulder and turned to

83

face me. "Gunner and I are going to make our mark on the world. Together."

A sob tore from my throat. "No! You can't take him away from me. I love him."

Mellie's eyes softened with pity. "He doesn't love you, Liddy."

"He doesn't love you either," I shot back, my voice sharp with desperation. "You've only known each other for less than twenty-four hours."

Mellie simply smiled—a sad, knowing smile. "Maybe not now," she admitted, "but he will in time."

She pulled an old boot box from the top shelf of her closet. Her jewelry. I knew then—she had planned this. This wasn't impulsive. This wasn't reckless. Mellie had been planning to leave me for a long time.

"I'm sorry it has to be this way, Liddy. But this is my only chance to get away. If I stay, Mama will—" She stopped. Her whole body went still.

"What?" I demanded, my pulse racing. "Mama will what?"

Mellie shook her head. "Never mind. You don't understand the pressure I'm under. You don't know what's expected of me as the firstborn."

Confusion twisted in my gut. "What do you mean? What are you talking about?"

Mellie's gaze turned guarded. "Ask Mama." She moved past me, heading for the stairs.

I grabbed her arm, desperate, pleading. "Mellie, don't leave me. Please."

She sighed, pressing a kiss to my forehead. "Be patient, Liddy. Your chance will come. I promise."

And then, just like that—she was gone.

I ran after her, out the door, down to the dock, my chest heaving, my lungs burning. But I was too late. My sister—my heart, my best friend, my blood—was already climbing into Gunner's boat.

And he was helping her. Not me. Her.

I gripped the dock piling, my vision blurred with heartbreak, my breath shattering in my chest.

They didn't even look back.

As the boat sped away into the gray horizon, something inside me broke. I fell to my knees, my body convulsing with sobs so deep, so raw, they felt like they would tear me apart.

And when I lifted my face to the sky, my broken whisper cracked in the thick summer air. "God, why did you let them take everything from me?"

Thirteen

2008

Sam arrives early the next day. Before sequestering himself in Mama's room, he helps me carry her boxes down to the living room. While he's upstairs working, I sort through her clothes. As I suspected, there's not a single item worth keeping—just threadbare dresses and shapeless housecoats, most too worn to donate. Even her clothes don't want to be remembered.

Around ten o'clock, I tap lightly on Mama's door, offering to help, but Sam refuses, determined to keep his surprise a secret.

He finally emerges around noon, bits of the yellow rose wallpaper stuck to his sweaty skin.

I serve lunch on the screen porch—homemade chicken salad, fresh fruit, and tall glasses of sweet tea.

"At least give me a hint," I say, spearing a strawberry with my fork.

Sam leans back, eyes on the ceiling fan, as if hoping inspiration might spin down with the breeze. "Think clean."

"Clean? Mama's room? You're not renovating. You're performing a miracle."

"The room isn't as bad as you make it out to be, Lydia.

You've built this up in your mind." His expression turns serious. "Tell me about your childhood. Was your mother abusive?"

I lower my gaze to my plate. "Not physically. It took me twenty years to understand that emotional and verbal abuse can cause just as much damage. She kept us here like prisoners. We rarely left Marsh Hollow. Now and then, she'd take us to Colton for supplies—when we needed new shoes or a winter coat. She made the rest of our clothes herself. Once we learned how to sew, we helped."

"I gather she homeschooled you," Sam said, his tone softer now, laced with sympathy.

"Yes. And she took that responsibility seriously. We studied every day of the year except Christmas, Easter, and New Year's Day."

"Did you ever try to get help?" Sam asks, shoveling in a forkful of chicken salad.

A flash of anger surges through me. "Get help for what? As a child, I didn't even realize there was a problem. I thought that was just how people lived. We had no exposure to other children, other families—except the kids we'd seen in town now and then. We begged Mama to let us go to school with them, but she convinced us we were special. That not everyone got to live in a place as sacred as Marsh Hollow."

"I'm sorry if I upset you," Sam says, setting down his fork and wiping his mouth. "I didn't know Aurelia well. She seemed like a nice lady. A little lonely, maybe. *Eccentric* is the word I'd use to describe her."

I've often wondered about Mama over the years. Was she still a midwife? Still a recluse? Still alive? "I imagine loneliness chips away at a person's sanity after a while."

"I imagine so," he says, his tone somber.

"There's so much about my childhood I don't understand. Now that my mother is gone, I guess I'll never know the truth." I search Sam's face, and the pity I find in his eyes makes me turn away. I don't want anyone feeling sorry for me—least of all him.

Standing, I gather up our plates. "Would you like a slice of Blossom's lemon pound cake?"

Sam rubs his belly. "Can I take a rain check? If I eat another bite, I'll need a nap."

I smile. "I'll save you a piece for later. Now, can I see your progress?"

He chuckles. "Not yet. Be patient. If all goes as planned, I'll finish the surprise and the brick steps by the end of the week."

A strange weight presses in my chest. Why am I so curious about his surprise? Why do I care what he's doing when I won't be living here?

After cleaning up from lunch, I retreat to the front porch with my sketch pad, where I spend the afternoon doodling, writing, and reflecting on the past. Around three o'clock, I glimpse Sam and Blossom hovering near the dumpster, deep in conversation, but I don't interrupt them. Whatever they're discussing is none of my business.

After numerous trips up and down the stairs, hauling out the old carpet remnants, Sam finally quits for the day around five o'clock.

I offer him dinner, which he politely refuses. "I'm going home for a hot shower and a stiff drink."

"You deserve both. Do you trust me not to peek at your progress?" I ask, glancing up at Mama's bedroom windows.

Sam's shoulders sag. "Obviously, I can't stop you, but I'd prefer for it to be a surprise."

"I wouldn't dare spoil it," I say with a reassuring smile.

I was joking with them, but resisting the temptation turns out to be harder than I imagined.

Sam returns at eight on Tuesday morning with buckets of paint and a floor sander.

I eye the floor sander. "Why are you refinishing the floors? I thought you said they were in good shape."

He winks. "Who says I'm refinishing them?" He disappears inside Mama's room, closing the door behind him.

I head to the kitchen for coffee, but the whine and vibration of the sander overhead sets me on edge. Retrieving my art supplies from my room, I make my way down to the marsh for the first time since I arrived.

I set up my easel in the exact spot in the hollow where Gunner and I had built our hideaway. The tranquility of the marsh washes over me, quieting my nerves, soothing something deep inside me. Clipping my watercolor sketchbook to the easel, I wet my brush, dribbling a few drops of water into the yellow-green paint pod. As I begin to paint, the familiar glide of brush against paper awakens something long dormant within me. Each stroke reconnects me to a part of myself I'd forgotten, a bridge to my past, a balm for my soul.

The years peel away, leaving me immersed in the pure, wordless dialogue between artist and canvas.

The sun is high in the sky when I break from my work. On the easel before me is a stunning rendition of the marsh hollow—a scene that has lived inside of me all these years.

You can take the girl out of the marsh, but you can't take the marsh out of the girl.

A load of bricks arrives that afternoon, and for the next three days, Sam splits time between rebuilding the front steps and completing my studio. *My studio?* When did I start thinking of the room as mine? Can a fresh coat of paint and a new purpose erase old memories?

89

Refusing to stop for lunch, Sam devours the egg salad and pimento cheese sandwiches I make for him between tasks. I offer to help with the brick steps, but though he's polite about it, I get the impression he prefers working alone.

With little to occupy my time in the house, I retreat to the marsh with my sketchbook and art supplies. I sketch herons and ospreys and the bald eagle who has taken up residence in the hollow during my absence. I paint cypress trees, their branches bowing toward the marsh grass, which is shedding its winter yellow for the vibrant greens of spring. With each stroke of my brush, I feel myself shrugging the weight of my past, much like a snake casting off its old skin—emerging renewed, vibrant, and wholly myself. Not the artist I once was, but as the one I have the talent to become.

Mid-afternoon on Friday, Sam seeks me out in the hollow. "What a sweet little spot. It's so much cooler here in the shade. And peaceful with the waves gently lapping the shore."

I smile up at him. "Isn't it heavenly? I just love it here."

"You belong here. You seem at one with the marsh." He peers over my shoulder at the watercolor on the easel—a lone oyster shell, tucked into the edge of the marsh grass, its iridescent blues and pinks glowing against its creamy belly. "That's amazing, Lydia. I had no idea you possessed such talent."

The appreciation in his voice is genuine, and warmth spreads through me. "Thank you. I haven't painted in years. I'm rediscovering my talent."

Sam's gaze shifts back to the oyster painting. "If this is your rusty work, I'd like to see what you can do when you're in full stride. Have you considered selling your paintings? I know an artist who owns a small gallery in Colton. I'd be happy to put you in touch with him."

My heart skips a beat at the thought of my work hanging in an art gallery. "Thanks, but I'm not ready for that. I'll keep it in mind though."

"Now that I've seen your work, I'm even more excited to introduce you to your new studio. Are you ready for a viewing?"

The words are on the tip of my tongue—*It's not my studio*—but I decide to pretend, just for the day, that I'm staying.

"I can hardly wait." I glance back at my painting. "I'm just about done here anyway."

Sam helps me gather up my supplies, and we return to the house together.

Blossom is waiting on the front steps. "Sam has outdone himself. I can hardly wait to see your face," she says, unburdening me of my easel.

Sam offers a sheepish smile. "I admit, I'm a little nervous."

I raise an eyebrow. "Really? Why?"

"There's a lot of pressure associated with remodeling someone's personal space."

"I've never thought about it, but I can see why. Do you ever get it wrong?"

He shrugs. "A time or two. But usually, we tweak things until we get it right. And we'll do that for you, too, if you're not completely satisfied."

After all his hard work and enthusiasm, I can't imagine telling him I'm dissatisfied—even if that's the case. "You can relax. This isn't my personal space."

"Not yet anyway. Hopefully, your new workspace will change your mind about selling," Sam says, motioning for us to go ahead of him into the house.

I deposit my art supplies on the living room floor, and we continue single file up the stairs.

At the top, Sam makes a drumroll sound. "Without further ado," he says, swinging the door open.

I am speechless at the transformation. The room gleams with pristine white paint covering the ceiling, walls, and trim, creating a seamless expanse of boundaries. The pickled floors provide a gentle contrast, their subtle tones infusing warmth to the space. In the far corner, a pale-blue leather armchair and worn pine hutch offer the only color. Even the adjacent bathroom has been painted white, making the vintage blue tile from the 1950s appear fresh.

"The furniture was Blossom's contribution," Sam says, following me around the room as I take it all in.

I glance over my shoulder at Blossom. "So that's what you two have been colluding about."

Blossom chuckles. "You know it! More treasures from my new favorite secondhand store."

I stop walking and turn to Sam. "It's amazing. If I wasn't thinking about staying before, I definitely am now."

Sam punches the air. "Yes!"

"I don't know how to thank you. I absolutely love it. You've accomplished the impossible. There's no trace of Mama left in this room."

A broad smile appears across his face. "It was my pleasure."

"You'll stay for dinner," I say, more of a command than an invitation. "It's the least I can do after everything you've done for me."

"Depends on what you're serving. I'm a picky eater." His tone is serious, but the smirk tugging at his lips gives him away.

"Either eggplant parmesan or lasagna. I waitressed in an Italian restaurant for over twenty years. I'm no professional chef, but I can hold my own in the kitchen."

"In that case, I wouldn't miss it. And for the record, I'll eat anything."

"Then lasagna it is," I declare.

He checks his watch. "I need to shower. How about I come back around six?"

"That'll be perfect."

After he and Blossom head downstairs, I remain in the doorway, taking in every detail of the transformed room.

It's not just a renovation. It's a reclamation. A blank canvas, not only for my art but for my future. For the first time since returning to Marsh Hollow, I feel something that looks and sounds a lot like belonging. Maybe I haven't just come back. Maybe I'm finally coming home.

I close the door gently behind me, the faint scent of paint still clinging to the air like a promise.

Fourteen

When I ask Blossom to join us for dinner, a look of mock horror crosses her face. "And interfere with your romantic evening? I wouldn't dare. This is your big chance to make your move on him."

I cut my eyes at her as I drop lasagna noodles in boiling water. "Shame on you, Blossom. Are you playing matchmaker again?"

"Maybe. I've been watching you two dance around each other this week. He's as smitten with you as you are with him. You sure would make a handsome couple."

Heat rises up my neck. The truth is, I've been looking forward to dinner with Sam all week. "Do you really think he's interested?"

"Indeed. It's as obvious as the fancy new art studio he created for you upstairs," Blossom says, pointing toward the ceiling. "He's a nice man, but no man is *that* nice. Now it's your turn to do something nice for him." She opens the pantry door, peers inside, then shuts it again with a little huff. "Please tell me you have a card table."

"Not that I know of. Maybe in the attic. Why?"

"Because, in addition to lasagna, you're gonna serve up a heaping of romance to Mr. Sam tonight."

"Blossom! I'm so out of practice in the romance department, I wouldn't even know where to start."

"It's simple. You set the scene and let him take the lead."

She leaves the kitchen, and I hear her plundering through the contents of Mama's sideboard.

"What're you looking for now?" I call over my shoulder from the stove.

Blossom reappears in the doorway. "Anything we can use to set the table?"

"You're wasting your time. You won't find anything like that in this house. I told you—Mama wasn't one for entertaining."

"I bet there's something in those boxes we saw in the attic."

I pause, remembering the ones labeled linens, crystal, and china. "Oh, right. I'd forgotten about those."

Blossom takes the wooden spoon from me and gives me a gentle nudge. "You go check the boxes. I'll finish here, then see if I have a card table in my bus."

"Yes, ma'am," I say, already heading for the stairs.

I have little experience with such things, but as I sift through the boxes, one thing becomes clear—these are not ordinary household goods. The linens are of the highest quality, the china elegant, the crystal gleaming as if cut from ice. Where did these treasures come from? Did they belong to my mother? My grandparents? Had someone in our family once lived a life of wealth and refinement—one that mama never spoke of?

I set aside a stack of delicate china plates, their creamy surfaces framed by an intricate green rim, the color reminiscent of new spring leaves. The pattern is elegant yet under-

ASHLEY FARLEY

stated, a fine lattice of vines and tiny blossoms circling the edge, a detail that speaks of refinement and old money.

Beneath the china, folded with meticulous care, I find a French tablecloth of the softest linen, embroidered with delicate white fleurs-de-lis along the edges. I unfold it, shaking it out, and imagine it once draped over a grand dining table, lit by candlelight, hosting elegant dinners with crystal clinking and hushed conversations.

But in my childhood, there had been no such dinners, no guests, no finery. Just the stark practicality of our everyday life, where meals were eaten in silence and beauty was something to be locked away in an attic.

Why had Mama kept these things hidden? And, more importantly—who had they belonged to?

I repack the items in the boxes and load up my arms with my treasures. I'm leaving the attic when I notice a much smaller box labeled *News Clippings.* I'm intrigued, and I long to explore the contents. But Sam will be here soon, and I still have to set the table, finish making dinner, and shower.

As I slowly make my way down the stairs, I glimpse Blossom, through the living room window, hanging vintage string lights from a low branch of the maple tree that overlooks the water.

"What're you doing?" I call, striding toward her across the lawn.

"Setting the scene, of course. I found a card table." She gestures at the folded wooden table leaning against the base of the tree. She eyes my loaded arms. "I see you had luck in the attic."

"I found some lovely things—too lovely for this house. I can't imagine who they belonged to." I give her a suspicious look. "Or did you put them there?"

"I most certainly did not," she huffs, indignant.

It's hard to say if she's telling the truth, and her tone gives nothing away. I decide not to press the matter further.

We set the table, the finishing touch a bouquet of green hydrangeas that Blossom seemingly conjures from thin air. With the soft glow of the string lights overhead and the gentle rustle of the marsh grass in the breeze, the scene is nothing short of magical. Satisfied, we head back to the kitchen to put the final touches on dinner.

As she tosses greens for a salad, Blossom says, "When are you going to finish writing your story? It tore my heart to pieces when Mellie ran off with Gunner. I can't imagine how hard that must have been for you."

I nod, my attention focused on spreading meat sauce on lasagna noodles. "And writing about it brings back all that heartache, which is why it's taking me so long to finish."

"I hope it's therapeutic too," Blossom says, dicing a cucumber.

"I guess it is. I'll know for sure once I finish the story."

Blossom covers the salad with plastic and places it in the refrigerator. "If you ever feel like talking about anything, I'm here."

"I know, and I appreciate the offer." I offer a sad, small smile. "Your presence is comfort enough. For now."

Sam arrives promptly at six, neatly dressed in khaki pants and a short-sleeved plaid shirt. His sandy hair, still damp from the shower, is combed back, and he carries the fresh scent of an ocean breeze on a clear day.

I've chosen a pale-blue knit dress that hugs my curves without being provocative. I wait for him in a rocker on the front porch. On the small table beside me sits an open bottle of red wine, two glasses, and a plate with a selection of artisanal Italian cheeses and gourmet crackers.

"Have you painted your first masterpiece in your new studio?" Sam asks, settling into the chair beside me.

I snicker as I pour wine into our glasses. "You've only been gone a couple of hours. Masterpieces take time."

"Good point." He takes a glass and holds it up to mine. "Shall we toast to you moving to Marsh Hollow?"

My smile fades. Today was the first time I've allowed myself to consider moving here. But I'm far from being ready to commit. "Why is it so important to you for me to stay? I get you're worried what a developer might do to the landscape, but I'm honestly leaning toward putting it on the market."

"Isn't it obvious to you by now?" A faint flush creeps up his cheeks. "I enjoy your company, Lydia. I don't want you to leave."

My chest swells at the quiet sincerity in his voice. "And I enjoy yours." I clink my glass to his. "I've gotten used to having you around this week. I'm going to miss you."

"I don't start my new project until Monday. That gives us the entire weekend to hang out, as the young folks say." He grins. "Are you free?"

My heart skips a beat at the prospect of spending time alone with him. "I'm free. What did you have in mind?"

"How do you feel about fishing?" he asks, watching me closely.

I tilt my head, considering. "Good question." Resting my head against the chair, I draw out the moment, pretending to contemplate. Then I roll my head to the side, meeting his gaze. "How about you fish, and I go along to cheer you on?"

He laughs out loud. "Fine by me, but won't you get bored?"

"*Bored?* Out on the water? Not a chance. I'll bring alone my sketch pad to capture the scenery."

Sam nods. "Fair enough. I have a couple of errands to run in the morning. How about if I pick you up around ten? After fishing, I'll take you to one of my favorite spots for a late lunch."

"I'd like that. What are you fishing for?"

"Rockfish are biting in the Rappahannock."

I stare out across the water. There are so many rivers and tributaries off the bay, I can't keep them all straight. "Is that far from here?"

He shakes his head. "Only about twenty minutes by boat."

While we finish our wine, I ask him more about fishing—not because I care about fish, but because I enjoy the smooth cadence of his voice and the way his face lights up when he talks about something he loves.

Our easy conversation carries over to dinner. Sam talks about his happy childhood growing up in Richmond, and I share the few good memories Mellie and I salvaged from ours.

After a while, I notice him studying me curiously. "What? Did I say something wrong?"

"Not at all. Nothing you say to me is *wrong*, Lydia. . . . I'm just curious about your sister. You don't talk much about her. I take it you two aren't close."

"That's an understatement. I haven't seen her in over twenty years."

His lips part slightly. "That's a long time. How does she feel about you selling the property?"

I shrug. "She doesn't know. She disclaimed her inheritance." My gaze drifts across the landscape—from the barn to the house to the open fields. "It's up to me to decide the fate of all this."

Sam lets out a low whistle. "That's an enormous burden to bear. All the more reason to take your time."

I nod, drawing in an unsteady breath. "Technically, she

relinquished all her rights to the property. But for whatever reason, I still feel like I need her approval."

As though sensing I'm on the verge of tears, Sam quickly shifts the conversation, rambling on about the new project he's starting next week.

After dinner, we stroll down to the hollow and sit on the beach, sinking our toes in the cool sand.

"I get why you love this spot." Sam stretches his legs out in front of him. "It's so secluded, I feel as though I'm part of nature, like an old cypress tree stump. I half expect a heron to land on my head any minute."

I laugh. "That would be a sight. But you're right. The rest of the world doesn't exist here. It's just us, the fish, and the birds."

His blue-gray eyes darken as he scans the hollow. "I can name a few other animals that might be lurking around too."

"Shh!" I press a finger to his lips. "I prefer not to think of those."

Sam takes my hand and brushes a kiss over my knuckles. A shiver rolls through me, and I release a breathy sigh.

"More?" he whispers.

"Yes, please," I murmur, my lips hovering near his.

His second kiss stirs something deep inside me, sending a jolt of electricity through my body.

Sam pulls back, his breath shallow. "I haven't been with a woman since my wife died. I haven't found anyone who interests me—until now." He places a hand on my cheek. "What I'm trying to say is, I'm rusty. I need you to be patient with me."

I let out a small laugh. "Then you're in good company. I've only been with one man in my life. And I've had just a handful of dates since him."

"Whew. That's a relief." He drags the back of his hand over his forehead, as if wiping away sweat. "Since we're in the same boat, let's just enjoy getting to know each other. We'll take it as it comes, one day at a time."

"One day at a time," I echo, resting my head on his broad shoulder.

An hour later, after seeing Sam off, I slip the last pages of my story under the door of Blossom's Celestial Cruiser. She'll have questions in the morning, and I'll answer them. But for the first time, I feel like I'm truly closing that chapter of my life —once and for all.

Fifteen

1987

Heartsick, I took to my bed for four days. Not only had I lost Gunner, but I'd also lost my sister. My only sibling. The one person who had endured every horrid moment of our childhood at my side. Mellie hadn't just abandoned me, leaving me alone with our crazy mama—she'd betrayed me. Stolen the boy I loved.

Visions of Gunner making love to my sister gnawed at my insides, stealing my appetite and robbing me of sleep. I cried until no tears were left, only getting up to use the bathroom.

When Mama returned at three o'clock in the afternoon on the fourth day, I braced myself for the inevitable tirade.

I padded downstairs in my pajamas and bare feet, the kitchen floor cool against my skin. I opened the back door, but I didn't rush outside to help with the groceries like I normally would have. Like I was expected to.

"What in the world, Lydia?" Mama hollered when she saw me in the doorway. "You look like the devil. Are you sick?"

"In a manner of speaking. I'm upset. Mellie ran away."

With paper shopping bags tucked under each arm, Mama

slammed the truck door and strode toward me. "What do you mean, she *ran away*?"

"She's gone," I said, my voice hollow. "And I don't think she's coming back."

Mama's face flushed a deep red, and the golden flecks in her hazel eyes—so like Mellie's—blazed with fury. "Why didn't you stop her?"

My mouth fell open. "As if I could. You know how she is. There's no stopping Mellie once she's made up her mind." I bit back the urge to remind her that my sister had inherited that stubborn streak from her.

Mama deposited the bags on the counter and reached into the cabinet for the spare cash can.

"I already checked," I said. "She didn't take any money."

Mama's body trembled with anger. "Then she had help. Who did she run away with? Was it a boy?"

My gaze dropped to the floor. "Yes, ma'am."

The cash can clattered onto the counter. Mama's voice rose. "Do you know this boy?"

"Yes, ma'am," I muttered.

"Who is he?" Mama demanded.

I shook my head. "I can't say."

Mama lunged, grabbing my chin in a bruising grip, forcing me to meet her eyes. "Tell me who he is," she hissed through clenched teeth.

I inhaled deeply, bracing myself. No matter what he had done to me, I would not betray Gunner. "It doesn't matter. They're long gone by now, and they're not coming back."

Mama's hand cracked hard across my cheek, the sting so sharp it brought tears to my eyes. "You're a disgrace." Grabbing me by the arm in an iron grip, she dragged me through the living room to the stairs. "Go to your room and don't come out until I say."

I took the stairs two at a time, flew down the hall, and

slammed the door behind me. Throwing myself onto the bed, I buried my face in the pillow to muffle my sobs. But for the first time since Mellie left, exhaustion overtook me, pulling me into a deep, dreamless sleep.

When I woke at dawn, my stomach gnawed with hunger.

Cracking my bedroom door, I peeked down the hall. Mama's door stood open, her bed neatly made. Either she'd risen earlier than usual, or she hadn't slept there last night. I tiptoed down the stairs, but the house was silent. Through the kitchen window, I spotted her truck in the driveway and a faint glow coming from the barn office.

I grabbed a loaf of bread and a jar of peanut butter and retreated to my room. I'd stay here until Mama calmed down —until I could figure out what to do next.

Hours later, when she finally emerged from the barn, her voice rang out from the bottom of the stairs. "Lydia! Come down to the living room. We need to talk."

My stomach clenched as I made my way downstairs.

Mama stood rigid in the center of the room, arms crossed, nodding toward the sofa for me to sit. She remained standing. "You'll begin your midwife training immediately."

My jaw hardened. "But I don't want to be a midwife."

Mama's expression darkened. "This isn't about what you want. Now go clean yourself up. You look dreadful."

Before, I never would have dared to talk back. But I wasn't the same girl anymore. I had known love. I had known betrayal. And I had survived.

Mellie's words echoed in my mind. *Be patient, Liddy. Your chance will come. I promise.*

I wouldn't fight Mama. Not yet. I'd play along, bide my time. Maybe Mellie and Gunner would send for me once they got settled in New York.

But even as the thought surfaced, it disintegrated. That wasn't going to happen.

Shoulders sagging under the weight of exhaustion, I trudged up the stairs to the bathroom, each step heavier than the last.

Why was I so tired all the time? Was it just the depression pressing me down, or was something else going on? Maybe a hot shower would clear my head.

Reaching for a fresh towel in the linen closet, my gaze landed on the box of tampons beside the spare rolls of toilet paper. I stared at it, a prickle of unease creeping through me. Then, a jolt of realization sent me racing to my room.

Grabbing my month-at-a-glance calendar off the desk, I flipped to August, counting the weeks with rising dread. My periods were like clockwork. I was ten days late.

I sank onto the bed as the truth crashed over me. Mama would beat the daylights out of me. Or would she? I was carrying a child, and Mama was a midwife dedicated to bringing new life into the world. If I became a midwife like she wanted, maybe she would let me keep my baby. But could I? Could I raise a child here, in this suffocating house, in this isolated existence that had nearly broken me? Could I trap my child the way I had been trapped?

A chill rippled through me. I had spent my entire life yearning for freedom. How could I now consider condemning my own child to the same cruel fate?

Falling back against the mattress, I stared at the ceiling, pressing my hands protectively over my belly. A new strength stirred inside of me—one that had nothing to do with defying Mama or Mellie or even Gunner.

The baby was mine. Conceived out of love, even if Gunner had never truly loved me back. He had left me with a parting gift. And I vowed, in that moment, that I would treasure it for the rest of my life.

Hope blossomed inside me during the days and weeks that followed. My breasts swelled, and nausea became a constant companion, but my resolve to keep the baby only deepened. For the first time in a long time, I didn't feel alone. The knowledge that a child was growing inside me gave me a sense of purpose, an anchor in a world that had always felt unsteady beneath my feet.

I wasn't ready to share my secret—not yet. I would wait until it was too late for anything to be done about it.

But one day toward the end of August, my body betrayed me. Mama heard me retching into the toilet and came to the bathroom door. "Are you sick?" she asked, her voice surprisingly gentle as she helped me up from the floor.

"Obviously," I muttered, turning to the sink. I splashed cold water on my face, grabbed a towel, and dried off before meeting her gaze in the mirror. "I'm pregnant."

Emotions rippled across Mama's face—bewilderment, shock, anger. Then her face hardened. "Who's the father?" she demanded.

When I didn't answer, Mama grabbed me by the shoulders and spun me around, her piercing eyes boring into me. I didn't have to tell her. She already knew.

A guttural laugh erupted from her throat, raw and bitter, echoing off the tiled walls. "Typical man!" Mama spat, her voice oozing with venom. "He chose the pretty sister and left the plain one to take care of his bastard child."

Her words hit their mark, sharp as a blade. I choked back a sob.

She waved a dismissive hand. "Never mind all that. It's up to you now to restore our family's reputation. We'll find just the right young man for you to marry."

I stared at her, aghast. "But I'm pregnant, Mama."

Her eyes narrowed, something unhinged glimmering behind them. "I'm leaving for a couple of days to deliver a baby. When I return, I'll take care of it. No one will ever know."

My stomach twisted with dread. "What do you mean, take care of it?"

She tilted her head, as if the answer should be obvious. "I'll abort it, of course."

Cold terror shot through me. "But it's too late! I'm too far along," I lied, desperation lacing my voice.

A glint of something cruel glimmered in her eyes. "I'm a midwife, Liddy. Doesn't matter how far along you are."

A creeping sense of horror overcomes me, pressing down like a force I couldn't shake. For the safety of my child and the sake of my sanity, I had no choice but to leave Marsh Hollow.

Sixteen

1008

"You naughty girl!" Blossom exclaims when I find her waiting in the kitchen with a fresh pot of coffee on Saturday morning. "How dare you leave me hanging like that!" She pulls out a chair and pats the seat. "Sit yourself down right now. I'm dying to hear how you got away from your evil mama."

I take the mug Blossom hands me and blow on the steaming coffee. "I hate to disappoint you, but there's not much else to tell. As soon as Mama left to visit her patient, I emptied the spare cash can and took off on foot toward Colton. I'd only gone a few miles when my shoes started rubbing blisters on my feet. I flagged down the next car that passed by, asking for a ride to wherever they were heading."

Blossom eases into the chair opposite me, her hands wrapped around her mug. "Lord help us, child. You could've been raped or murdered." She dabs at her eyes with a napkin. "Bless your little heart. You were just a baby, with no real-world experience. How were you supposed to know how dangerous hitchhiking is?"

I cast my eyes toward the ceiling. "God was looking out for me. The young couple who picked me up—Giorgio and

Carmela Mancini—saved my life. They had just opened an Italian restaurant in Richmond. They offered me a job and a place to live until after the baby came, when I could afford an apartment of my own. As the saying goes, the rest is history."

Blossom's smile stretches slow and tender. "Despite all you went through, you turned out pretty special. Now tell me about your relationship with Nate."

I stare down into my coffee cup, slowly tracing the rim with my fingertip. "Sadly, despite everything I've sacrificed for him, we've never been close. He resents me for keeping the truth about his father from him."

Blossom's brows lift. "You mean you never told him who his father is?"

I shake my head. "We've been arguing about it for years. We had a terrible fight on Christmas Eve, and we haven't spoken since."

"Have you tried calling him?"

"No. He had too much to drink that night, and he said some horrible things to me." I tighten my grip on my mug. "Call me stubborn, but he owes me an apology."

Blossom fixes me with a stern look, the kind that makes me feel like a child caught red-handed. I lower my gaze.

"Being a parent means choosing love over pride, even when it hurts. And right now, love's the only thing that'll bring your boy back." She tilts her head, studying me. "What's really stopping you from telling Nate the truth about his father?"

My head snaps up. "Isn't it obvious? I'm protecting my sister's marriage."

She cuts her eyes at me. "With all due respect, Goldie Girl, that makes no sense. You were with Gunner first. Your sister is the one who stole your boyfriend." She slides her chair closer and lowers her voice. "Wanna know what I think?"

I force a smile, swiping at my damp eyes. "You're going to tell me anyway."

"Mm-hmm. I think you're afraid Gunner will take Nate away from you the way he took Mellie?"

I stiffen. "That's not fair. Gunner didn't take Mellie. She stole him from me. And Nate? He's *my* son. I raised him on my own. I've been there for every scraped knee, every school project, every heartbreak. Don't you dare suggest I'm afraid of losing him." But the tremble in my voice gives me away. Because maybe—just maybe—I am.

Blossom places her hand over mine. "You love your son, and your heart was in the right place. But a child isn't a prize to be won or a secret to be kept. A child belongs to both parents, whether or not we like it." She squeezes my fingers. "You can keep Nate all to yourself, but love doesn't work like that. Love isn't about possession—it's about giving. And if you love that boy, truly love him, you'll let him decide what having a father means to him." Her gaze falls on me. "You're not losing your son, sweetheart. You're just giving him a chance to know the whole of himself."

When she wraps an arm around me, I collapse into her side and cry until there's nothing left to give.

She quietly hands me a fresh tissue. "Feel better?"

"I guess," I say, blowing my nose. "Writing the story helped. I understand why people say writing is good therapy."

Blossom leans back, her expression turning thoughtful. "Now that you've got the simple part behind you, are you ready to dig in?"

"What do you mean?"

"You've written about the past. Now you need to reconcile with it. If you want real closure, you need to make amends with your sister."

"And just how do you suggest I do that?" I rub my temples, frustration bubbling to the surface.

"You can start by reaching out to her. Do you have any idea how to get in touch with her?"

I nod slowly. I've considered it more times than I can count. "Through her website. She's a famous jewelry designer. Melanie Stone. Ever heard of her?"

Blossom's mouth drops open. "Who hasn't heard of Melanie Stone? I admire her work myself." Her eyes brighten as if a lightbulb just flicked on. "Wait a minute. I'm putting this all together now. Melanie Stone is married to Gunner Stone. *The* Gunner Stone, famous music producer."

"He's the one."

"Call her! Email her!" Blossom's voice bubbles with excitement. "What do you have to lose?"

"I can't. I have no internet and barely any cell service."

"You're welcome to visit my Command Center. The internet is light-years fast, Goldie. No dial-up tones, no beeping—just pure, instant magic. And the cell reception? Clear as Alexander Graham Bell!"

I laugh. "Maybe later. I'm not sure I'm ready for such a drastic step."

I glance at the wall clock. If I hurry, I have time to run up to the attic and still be ready when Sam arrives at ten. "I have plans with Sam later. What does one wear to go fishing?"

Blossom stands and gives me a playful twirl, my robe flaring out around me. "Cute Bermuda shorts to show off your pretty legs. A light-colored tee to keep you cool—pastel pink or pale blue. And of course, a sassy sun hat."

"But I don't own a sassy sun hat."

Blossom lifts a finger. "Wait right here. I have just the thing in my bus," she says, already bolting out the door.

But even as she disappears, my thoughts are already drifting. That box in the attic—the one labeled *News Clippings*. What could possibly be inside?

I have to find out.

111

Seventeen

I drag the box over to the window, where a patch of sunlight spills across the attic floor. Kneeling beside it, I tear through the crackling packing tape and fold back the flaps, releasing a cloud of dust, thick with the scent of aged paper. Inside are stacks of folded newspapers, their pages yellowed and brittle with time.

The topmost paper takes my breath away. Staring back at me from the wedding announcements section of the *Richmond Times-Dispatch* is my mother—no older than twenty, the very image of my sister. Dressed in a creamy satin and lace wedding gown, she gazes out with a serene smile, poised and radiant. Beneath the photograph, the caption reads:

Anna Aurelia Malone marries Senator Everett Meyer in wedding fit for Royalty.

How can this be? My father was a US senator?

I sit down on my bottom, not caring that my shorts are white and the floor is filthy. Sorting through the articles chronicling my parents' early years together, I find entire newspaper sections and carefully clipped columns from the *New York Times*, *Washington Post*, and *Miami Herald*.

In addition to the newspapers, there are a few magazines, such as *Vogue* and *Harper's Bazaar*, featuring articles about the elegant young senator's wife. The June 1967 edition of *Town and Country* magazine did a spread on Mama at Briarwood Hall—my father's hundred-acre horse farm in Middleburg.

I'm positively floored. I'm certain Mama never mentioned a horse farm in Middleburg. Who lives there now? Are my paternal grandparents still alive?

I long to devour every word, but with Sam arriving soon, I skim the articles instead.

In the photographs, my socialite Mama is dressed in couture—Chanel, Christian Dior, Yves Saint Laurent—at lavish parties, political rallies, and White House events. But as I study the grainy images, something feels off. She doesn't look poised or confident. She looks like a deer in the headlights.

In contrast, my father stands tall with an air of elegance, his posture rigid, his handsome face set in a stern expression, exuding an undeniable aura of superiority. He appears much older than Mama. At least forty years old, if I had to guess.

The newspapers are stacked in order, each headline a step deeper into the past. Near the bottom, I find the reports of my father's death in January 1971.

January 1971. Mama would've been four months pregnant with me. I'd always believed my father had died after I was born.

From The Associated Press:

Senator Everett Meyer Dies in Tragic Car Crash

MIDDLEBURG, VA—Senator Everett Meyer, a prominent political figure and heir to the esteemed Meyer family estate, was killed late last night when his vehicle veered off a narrow stone bridge and plunged into Blackwater Creek. Authorities believe the senator may have fallen asleep at the wheel while driving home from Washington, D.C. The wreckage was discovered early this morning by a passing motorist, who noticed a section of the bridge's stone barrier missing. Emergency responders recovered the senator's body from the submerged vehicle, and an investigation into the cause of the crash is ongoing.

I read on, learning about the enormous speculation surrounding the tragic car accident. The police blamed the incident on icy roads, but some reporters claimed he'd been drinking and others speculated he was having an affair. My mother, who had apparently suffered from postpartum depression after Mellie's birth, had become something of a recluse, living full-time at Briarwood Hall.

And then, at the bottom of the stack, on the front page of the *National Inquirer*, a bold headline jumps out at me.

Everett Meyer's Family Rumored to be Part of Secret Society.

My pulse quickens as I flip to the article.

Inside sources suggest that my father's family were long-time members of the Dominion Society—and that he was involved in something nefarious. Some even claim the Dominion Society staged his death to cover up the evidence.

I'm so immersed in the articles, I don't hear Sam's horn at first. But the ringing of the doorbell lulls me out of my trance and pulls me back to the present. I hurriedly stack the newspapers back into the box, my hands trembling. With one last glance at the haunting image of my mother in her wedding gown, I close the flaps and rise to my feet, brushing off my shorts. Sam rings the bell again, and I take a steadying breath before heading downstairs, my mind still reeling from everything I've just uncovered.

Despite having lived on the water during my youth, I've only ridden in a boat a few times—all with Gunner. I perch on the bow with my sketch pad while Sam tends to his fishing rods at the stern. Seagulls dive around us, snatching fish from the water, but the page remains blank in my lap. My thoughts are too tangled to focus.

Why had my mother married a much older man? Was my father's death truly an accident, or had he been drinking that night? Was he having an affair? If so, was the other woman with him? Did she die in the crash, and the Dominion Society cover it up?

And that graffiti painted on my kitchen wall—did the *D* stand for Dominion?

A shadow crosses my line of sight, and I'm surprised to see Sam standing before me. "Are you okay? You were off on another planet."

"I'm fine. Just thinking." My gaze shifts to the back of the boat where he's pulled his lines out of the water. "Did you catch anything?"

He shakes his head. "I'm not feeling it today." He sits down beside me. "I'd rather talk about what's bothering you."

I take a deep breath, trying to steady my voice. "I . . . um . . . I found something in the attic this morning. A box containing newspaper articles about my parents." I rub my temples, trying to piece my thoughts together. "There's a lot I still don't understand, but... my father wasn't just some guy. He was a US senator." I continue on, telling him about the accident and whispers of conspiracy that followed. But I leave out the part about the secret society. That part feels too big, too off-limits, too dangerous to say out loud yet.

Sam leans back, his arm resting on the seat behind me. "No wonder you're unusually quiet. That's a lot to absorb."

I nod. "But while I have more questions than answers now, I feel connected to Mama in a way I never did when she was alive. Seeing those sad photographs of her, hearing about her postpartum depression, softened me toward her. She was human, with her own problems. She wasn't just the harsh, unyielding woman I remember—she was struggling in ways I never understood." I stare out at the water, my mind racing. "I can't shake the feeling that something about my father's death changed her. That whatever happened that night shaped the way she raised us."

"Is there anyone who can give you some answers?" Sam asks gently.

My sister may know more about our family history, but I'd hate to spoil a beautiful day by talking about Mellie. "If you're done fishing, can we go to lunch now? I'm starving."

"Sure thing," Sam says, getting to his feet. "We have a short ride. Hopefully, the crowd will be dying down by the time we get there."

Merroir, a member of the Rappahannock Oyster Company restaurant chains, is in Topping, Virginia, just off the Rappahannock River. They consider themselves a tasting room, serving small plates of seafood, either raw or cooked on an outdoor grill.

Sam and I devour plates of raw oysters and sip chilled sauvignon blanc on their patio at a table with an orange umbrella. Afterward, we spend hours winding along the banks of the Corrotoman River and Carter's Creek, admiring the grand homes and their stunning waterfront views.

Late afternoon, we're headed back across the bay when Sam calls above the hum of his motor, "I picked up two tuna steaks at the seafood market this morning, hoping you'd join me for dinner."

I peer at him over my sunglass frames. "You bought fish? You didn't have much faith in your chances of catching any, did you?"

He laughs out loud. "I was an Eagle Scout. I'm always prepared."

I smile. "That explains a lot. No wonder you're so resourceful. And I accept your invitation. Tuna sounds delicious." Today has been a blessed respite from the memories and unanswered questions that haunt Marsh Hollow. And I'm not ready for it to end.

Sam's cottage is charming, with gray siding, black shutters, and a bold red front door. The interior is tidy yet inviting, handsomely decorated with a well-balanced mix of antiques and modern furnishings.

We eat on the porch, overlooking the water. Sam plates up perfectly seared tuna alongside warm cornbread and a crisp Asian salad tossed in sesame teriyaki dressing. As the sun dips below the horizon, we stretch out in his hammock, strung between two sturdy trees in the yard, and gaze up at the starry sky.

We don't talk much, each of us lost in our own thoughts, but the silence between us feels natural.

On Sunday morning, Sam takes me to a quaint, non-denominational chapel in a small, off-the-beaten-track town. The preacher, a robust black man in his forties, delivers a heartfelt sermon about forgiveness—as though he were talking directly to me.

We gorge ourselves on brunch at The Tide's Inn, then migrate to the Adirondack chairs on the lawn to watch the boats go by.

"What's on your agenda for the week?" Sam asks, his eyes closed, face tilted to the sun.

"I'm hoping to spend some time in my new studio organizing my art supplies . . ."

"And?"

Reluctantly, I say, "And I'm considering continuing with minor renovations."

He grins, but his eyes remained closed. "I hope this means you're staying for good."

I nudge his arm. "Stop! You know I haven't decided yet. But I admit I'm inspired by the improvements. I see no harm in making a few more changes."

Sam rolls his head on the back of the chair to look at me. "Such as?"

"Cleaning the cedar paneling in the alcove, like you suggested. Since my wonderful new art studio is making the rest of the upstairs look dingy, I may paint the hallway and give my bedroom a makeover."

"Good for you! What will you do with your sister's room? You could turn it into a small sitting room."

"I'll leave that room alone for now." The mention of my sister's room reminds me of what lies ahead. Once the weekend ends, it's back to reality for me. My end-of-May deadline is fast approaching. I need to decide whether to sell the house. The newspaper articles have opened a can of worms for me. And I won't feel comfortable turning my family's property over to a stranger until I learn more about our past.

Eighteen

A scrumptious aroma greets me when I return home from my date with Sam. Entering the kitchen, I find Blossom stirring ingredients into a sleek standing mixer—one I'm certain didn't belong to Mama.

"I won't ask you where you got the mixer," I say with a snicker.

She twirls her spatula like it's a magic wand, flashing a mischievous grin.

I peer into the mixing bowl. "What're you making anyway?"

"Kitchen sink cookies," she says, dumping in a cup of coconut.

I swipe a finger through the dough and zap it into my mouth. "This is yummy. What's in it?"

"Everything but the kitchen sink," she says, and we both laugh.

I sneak another taste, sucking the batter off my finger with a satisfied pop. "I'm gonna run up to the attic while you finish up. I have something to show you. I'll be right back."

I return a moment later, breathless from my quick trip up two flights of stairs. While Blossom slides the last batch of cookies into the oven, I spread the news clippings across the table in neat, organized stacks.

Together, we pore over each article, discussing details as we go. This time, I absorb more than before. I learn my father was in his second term as a senator. That he was an only child and both his parents—my paternal grandparents—were deceased. That Mama stood to inherit a fortune, including Briarwood Hall, upon his death.

By the time we finish, it's past midnight. We've downed an entire pot of decaf coffee and eaten more kitchen sink cookies than I care to admit.

Leaning back in my chair, I rub my swollen belly. "Well? What do you think?"

Blossom's gaze drifts past me to the watercolors we'd hung over the graffiti. "My gut reaction? This secret society is the key to everything." She jabs a finger toward the wall. "And the people who broke in here and painted that mess? They're connected to it."

A chill snakes down my spine. "What makes you think that?" I ask, already suspecting where she's going with this—but needing to hear her say it out loud.

Pushing herself out of the chair, she strides over and yanks the watercolors down, revealing the tangled letters—*D* and *V* —stark against the faded paint. "I have a sneaking suspicion that *D* stands for Dominion."

I get up and stand beside her. "I was wondering about that too. But what does the *V* stand for?"

"Could be anything. Five? The fifth?"

"Or another word beginning with *V*," I murmur.

Blossom turns to me, reaching into the deep pocket of her dress and withdrawing a slip of paper. "You need answers. And there's only one person who may be able to give them to you."

She presses the paper in my hand. "I looked up your sister's contact information. My Command Center is at your disposal whenever you're ready to reach out."

I glance down at the paper. Written in print as neat as a typewriter are the phone number for Melanie Stone Designs and a generic email address for general inquires.

"Unfortunately, I think you're probably right," I say with a heavy sigh, slipping the paper into my pocket. "I can no longer put off the inevitable."

———

Early Monday morning, with a steaming cup of coffee in hand, I step outside, wandering to the edge of the yard near the fields where the cell service is strongest. I take a deep breath before tapping in the number from the slip of paper Blossom gave me.

"Melanie Stone's office. Who's calling, please?" The receptionist's tone is clipped, all business.

I hesitate for a fraction of a beat. "Lydia Meyer. I'm her sister."

The receptionist's tone brightens with curiosity. "Really? Cool! I didn't know Melanie had a sister. Hang on just a sec. Let me get her for you."

I remain on hold for nearly five minutes before the receptionist returns, her tone now impersonal and brisk, as if eager to get rid of me. "I'm sorry to keep you waiting. Melanie is in an important meeting and can't be disturbed. I can take a message."

The enthusiasm from earlier has vanished. Melanie isn't in a meeting. She just doesn't want to speak to me.

I rattle off my contact information, keeping my voice even, then hang up.

A seed of determination takes root in my gut. *She won't get rid of me that easily.*

I wait an hour before trying again. I'm sitting on the porch, and surprisingly, the call goes through. Apparently, the cell service depends on the weather, the wind direction, and maybe even the phase of the moon. But today, the stars align.

This time, a different receptionist answers. When I provide my name, her tone turns clipped. "I'm sorry. Mrs. Stone is out to lunch with clients. I'm not sure when she'll be back," she says, and promptly hangs up without asking for my number.

I call right back. "You hung up on me before I could leave my information," I say, irritation creeping into my voice.

"Mrs. Stone already has the number," the receptionist snaps, then ends the call again.

I stare at the phone in disbelief. Before I can decide what to do next, a silver sedan barrels down the gravel driveway, kicking up dust, and screeches to a halt in front of the porch.

The driver's door flies open and out strides a bowling ball of a woman in a black pantsuit, her gray hair pulled into a severe bun. She moves with purpose, her ample hips swaying as she approaches.

"Hey there!" she calls in a warm, country drawl. "I'm Marge Crenshaw. I work with Arthur Pendleton. You must be Lydia Meyer."

"Yes, ma'am. What can I do for you?"

Marge peers at me over the top of her oversized bug-eye sunglasses. "Well, aren't you a sight for sore eyes? It's nice to finally meet you in person."

I offer a polite smile, unsure how to respond. "Likewise. What brings you out here?"

She waves a file folder in the air. "Got some papers for you to sign, authorizing us to move forward with probating your mama's property. We sent a duplicate to your place in Richmond, but when Arthur mentioned you were staying at Marsh Hollow, I figured I'd save us both some trouble and bring another copy."

"Of course. I'd be happy to sign." An idea sparks in my mind—this might be my chance to learn more. "Arthur mentioned sending someone from the sheriff's office to talk to me about my mother's death. I'm still waiting. If there's anything you know . . ."

Marge presses her lips into a thin line. "Lord, I wish I didn't. Still keeps me up at night." She flaps a hand in front of her face, fanning herself. "Do you mind if we sit a minute? It sure is warm out today."

"Not at all. Come on up," I say, gesturing to the porch. "Can I get you something to drink?"

"Nah, I'm fine. I can't stay but a minute."

She settles into a rocker, waiting for me to do the same before handing over the folder. I follow her instructions, signing where needed, then pass it back.

"Now," she says, folding her hands over her lap. "What is it you want to know about the case?"

"Anything, really. Arthur told me next to nothing," I say, my voice edged with frustration. "Not even about the home invasion."

"Can't blame poor Arthur," Marge says, removing her sunglasses and wiping the lenses with the hem of her suit jacket. "After your sister so abruptly disclaimed her inheritance, he worried it might scare you off too. He's just trying to do right by your mother—make sure the property ends up in good hands." She slides her sunglasses back onto her face. "The mail lady found her, you know?"

My eyes widen. "No! I didn't know."

"Well, technically, that's not entirely true," Marge clarifies. "The carrier got concerned when the mail started piling up and called the sheriff's office for a wellness check. The sheriff broke in and found her. She'd been dead for a while."

My stomach turns. "How long?"

Marge's stubby legs pump the rocking chair. "Several weeks." She pulls a tissue from her jacket sleeve and dabs at her nose, as if the memory still carries a scent. "The sheriff had the house sealed off as a crime scene for months. We did our best to straighten up her room before you arrived. But the rest of the house? I'm sorry to say, we didn't have the time."

"That explains why her room was empty."

Marge nods. "It was bad, honey. That mattress where she lay dead for all those weeks? We had to get rid of it. We boxed up her clothes and things. I assume you found those in the closet?"

I nod. "Yes. Thanks."

It suddenly hits me—Mama had been married to a wealthy man. Could she have owned expensive jewelry? Hidden something valuable in the house? Is that what the intruders were searching for?

"When did she die?" I ask. "No one ever told me."

"December fifteenth." Marge sighs. "I'd just gotten back from my book club's Christmas luncheon when I heard the news."

I blink in disbelief. "She died in December? And I didn't find out until April?"

Marge exhales, as if bracing herself for my reaction. "It took us some time to track you down. There wasn't a trace of either of you in the house—no birth certificates, no health records, nothing."

My breath catches. "Then how did you finally find us?"

"One of our sheriff's deputies . . ." She clears her throat, coughing into her hand. "Well, let's just say he was obsessed with this case. He reached out to the local midwives. One of them is a fan of your sister's jewelry. He was able to track Melanie down through her company."

"What about the intruders? Were they looking for something specific, or was it just a random break-in? I understand the coroner ruled her death natural causes, but she was only sixty-four. Are they certain the break-in wasn't related, that the intruders didn't murder her?" I asked, gripping the arms of my chair to steady myself.

Marge lets out a slow breath. "All good questions, Lydia. And none that I can answer." She leans forward, lowering her voice. "You can talk to the sheriff. But from what I hear, he found nothing. He's already closed the case."

As she stands to go, Marge leaves a business card on the table beside me. "If you have any more questions, or you just want to talk, feel free to reach out."

I get up and walk Marge to her car. "One more thing before you go. Do you know anything about the graffiti on the kitchen wall?"

The color drains from Marge's face. "Our crew was supposed to remove that."

"The letters are arranged in such a specific manner, almost like a seal. Do they represent something? Maybe a secret society?"

Marge glances around nervously, then lowers her voice and leans in. "Forget you saw it, Lydia. I'll have someone come by this afternoon to take care of it."

"No need," I say casually. "I'm planning to paint that room anyway."

Marge hesitates, her hand resting on the open car door. "Good," she says, her voice firm. "It's best not to dwell on things that don't concern you."

A shiver runs down my spine. "But it does concern me, doesn't it? This is my childhood home. My family's legacy. My mother died here."

Marge doesn't respond. She just climbs into the driver's seat and starts the engine.

As she pulls away, I stand frozen in the driveway, the business card pressed in my palm. Marge knows more than she's letting on—her odd behavior confirms it. Something sinister happened in this house. To my mama. And whatever Marge is afraid of . . . I am now caught up in it.

Nineteen

A sharp crack of lightning, followed by a booming clap of thunder, jolts me awake. Heart pounding, I throw back the covers and stagger to the window. Is it my imagination? Or is that a person—a drenched figure—emerging from the woods on the far side of the fields? Mellie. Rain slicks her deep red hair to her head, her white nightgown soaked and clinging as she trudges through the muddy field, a ghostly figure moving toward the house.

She's carrying something—her arms wrapped around it, shielding it from the driving rain.

A voice, soft and raspy but unmistakably my mama's, whispers near my ear, *"The secrets were never meant to stay buried."*

I clamp my hands over my ears. "Go away. I can't hear you! You're dead." Spinning away from the window, I squeeze my eyes shut and slide down the wall to the floor.

When I finally dare to open my eyes, relief washes over me —it was only a dream. But the memory of it lingers. Mellie had been returning from the cemetery. That eerie, forbidden place in the woods had haunted me as a child, filling my nights with nightmares that left me breathless in the dark. But Mellie had been obsessed. She had written about it in her little notebook.

I can see it in my mind as clearly as if it were yesterday—a small, spiral-bound notebook with a black cover, its corners bent from constant handling. She had stolen it from the general store in Colton, tucking it beneath her dress while I stood watch. She never let me see what she wrote inside, snapping it shut the moment I got too close. Whatever was written on those pages, she'd guarded fiercely, as if it held secrets too dangerous to share.

Another streak of lightning flashes, illuminating the room for an instant. Then everything goes dark. The hall light flickers out, and the steady hum of the air conditioner falls silent.

I will never be able to live at Marsh Hollow permanently until I face my fears and make peace with the past and all the secrets it holds. And Mellie's notebook is as good a place as any to start.

I crawl over to my bed and pull myself to my feet. I've been gone for twenty-two years, but I still know this house well enough to feel my way across the hall in the dark. Although with the power out and despite the frequent flashes of lightning, I would need a flashlight to properly search her room. There may still be one in the kitchen junk drawer where we used to keep them, but I'd just as soon as wait until morning.

I curl into a ball on Mellie's bed, and as the storm rages outside, childhood memories crash over me like waves battering a boat in rough seas. The way the house seemed to breathe at night, floorboards groaning under the t of something unseen. The whispers I swore I heard coming from Mama's room when I pressed my ear to the door, though no one was ever inside. Mellie shaking me awake in the dead of night, her face pale, eyes wild. "I saw someone at the edge of the field," she whispered. "They were just standing there, watching the house."

The hushed arguments between Mama and Mellie when they thought I was asleep. "You'll do as you're told. You are the firstborn. You are bound by obligation."

Bound by obligation to do what?

And now, lying in the dark, I realize something I was too young to understand back then—Mama wasn't just strict. She was afraid. Always afraid.

But of what? Or who?

I wake at the first light of dawn and tear Mellie's room apart, rummaging through the few things my sister left behind. Mostly old clothes—a down coat with frayed cuffs, a pair of muddy boots shoved in the closet. Her drawers hold scraps of the past—shorts, T-shirts, and jeans she outgrew a long time ago. We never had much to begin with, and Mellie took her most valued possessions with her when she left.

Her bedside table drawer is filled with chunks of sea glass in a variety of shapes and hues—blue, green, rose, and purple. I pick up a smooth, sea-green piece, turning it over in my palm. The edges have been worn soft by time, but the surface is still cool against my skin.

When it slips from my fingers and clinks against the floor, I lean down to retrieve it. That's when I notice it. Near the headboard, one floorboard juts up slightly higher than the rest. My pulse quickens. I slither under the bed on my belly like a snake, pressing my fingers against the uneven board. It shifts under the pressure.

A hidden compartment.

I hesitate, my imagination conjuring spiders, mice, or worse, lurking inside. Squeezing my eyes shut, I reach into the darkness, exhaling in relief when my fingers land on something solid. I pull out Mellie's spiral-bound notebook, setting it aside and feeling around the space again. My fingers brush against something else. I withdraw a small, rectangular box—caramel-colored leather, smooth with age. I lift the lid, and inside, nestled like a forgotten secret, is a single rusty key.

A key and a cemetery—how could they possibly be connected? Was it just a coincidence Mellie hid them together, or had she discovered something more?

Crawling from beneath the bed, I thumb through the notebook, line after line of names—our ancestors, their birth and death dates carefully recorded in Mellie's precise hand-writing. Toward the back, the entries shift. Family trees meticulously sketched out, linking generations of Malones through birth and marriage.

My gaze shifts back to the leather box on the floor beside me. Something tells me Mellie's entries and the key are connected. The key may unlock something hidden in the cemetery.

Ironically, after a lifetime of fearing the dreadful place, I can hardly wait to get there. Throwing on some clothes, I bolt from the house, the notebook and key clutched tightly in my hands.

Branches scratch my bare arms as I push through the overgrown path. Over two decades have passed since I was last here, but the way to the cemetery is etched in my memory. I pause outside the main gate—heavy wrought iron, rusted with time, its bars now completely covered by overgrown vines. When I grip the handle and push, the gate resists, groaning in protest before giving way with a slow, grating creak.

My pulse quickens, a primal urge clawing at my chest. Should I leave now before it's too late? What if I find something that endangers my life? Is my life already in danger? I'm being ridiculous. Who would want to hurt me? Besides, I've never come this far before, and I'm not turning back now.

The graves stretch in two orderly rows, vanishing into the depths of the woods. As I walk between them, I notice the limestone markers are nearly identical—each one etched with a name, every last one a Malone by birth or marriage. At the end of the path, looming in the dappled shadows, stands a massive bronze figure.

And this creepy statue, a weird-looking man, Mellie had said about him.

The statue of Ambrose Bartholomew Malone stands tall and imposing, his sharp features captured in metal—his receding hairline, a prominent hawkish nose, and a gaze that seems to follow me. He wears a high-collared jacket, the folds of fabric expertly sculpted, an ascot knotted neatly at his throat. One hand rests on the hilt of a cane, the other tucked behind his back, giving him an air of quiet authority. Engraved at the base of the statue are the words:

AMBROSE BARTHOLOMEW MALONE
1587 – 1645
The Grand Founder
The First Among Us. Forever in Power.

"The Grand Founder," I murmur. "Founder of what? The Dominion Society?"

Something else draws my attention—a subtle seam in the back, where his long tailcoat flares slightly. I crouch down, running my fingers along the metal. The folds of his coat are sculpted in lifelike detail, but one section feels hollow beneath my touch. With a firm press, a hidden panel clicks open.

In the distance, Blossom's voice echoes through the woods. "Lydia! Lydia! Where are you? Come quickly! We're under a tornado warning."

The key weighs heavily in my pocket as I glance between the statue and the direction of Blossom's voice. Facing a tornado feels far less terrifying than unearthing the secrets buried in this haunted place.

I click the compartment door back into place and flee the cemetery.

Blossom stands in the middle of the field, turning in frantic circles, still calling my name. When she spots me emerging from the woods, she yells for me to hurry, and we sprint together toward the house, the wind whipping around us.

Inside the kitchen, I yank open the pantry door and lift the trapdoor hidden beneath the shelves. A set of folding stairs creak as we descend into the cramped basement below. The air is thick with the scent of earth and mildew.

I shiver, but not from damp. "The power's still out. How did you hear about the tornado warning?"

"Power's not out in the Celestial Cruiser." Blossom removes a pink bandana from her pocket and mops the beads of sweat off her face. "Where were you, Goldie Girl? I was terrified."

"In the family cemetery." My voice wavers as I tell her about Mellie's obsession with the cemetery, my discovery of her notebook and key in her room, and my growing belief that clues about my family's past may be hidden in the statue.

"Ambrose Bartholomew Malone," I murmur. "Born in 1587 and died in 1645. He must have been born in England. If he's my grandfather, that's too many greats to count."

"Could be a great-uncle," Blossom suggests.

I nod. "Could be. He was called The Grand Founder. Wonder what he was the founder of. On the statue below *The Grand Founder* is written: *The First Among Us. Forever in Power.*"

"Now I'm curious. Sounds like he was a man of great influence."

"Once these storms move on, I'm going back to the cemetery," I say firmly. "I have to know what's hidden in that statue."

"Not alone, you're not," Blossom says, folding her arms. "I'm going with you."

A knot squeezes in my stomach. "You think I'm in danger." It's not a question.

She hesitates. "I don't know. The graffiti on the kitchen wall feels intentional—not like the kind you find spray-painted on a building or scrawled under an overpass. And honestly? I wouldn't take the medical examiner's cause of death at face value either."

I exhale sharply. "You don't think she died of natural causes?"

Blossom shrugs. "You said it yourself—she was only sixty-four. If those intruders scared her into having a heart attack, it would've shown up on the autopsy."

My throat thickens. "You're right. Things aren't adding up. But I can't let you go to the cemetery with me. I won't put your life in danger too."

Blossom huffs, hands on her hips, then gives me a pointed look—a silent reminder that she's already dead.

Twenty

An hour passes before we summon the courage to poke our heads through the trapdoor. To our relief, the storm has moved out, and the sky stretches overhead in a brilliant cerulean blue, unbroken by clouds. Stepping out the kitchen door, we scan the farm for damage—fallen trees, debris, any sign of destruction. But everything appears untouched.

"Looks like we got lucky this time," Blossom says, marveling at the unscathed landscape.

I tilt my face toward the warm spring sun. "It's too nice out to go back into the woods. Or to spend the day cooped up painting walls. I'm in the mood to plant something. Flowers, maybe. Containers for the front porch. Do you think there's a garden center in Colton?"

"I'm certain of it. On the outskirts of town. I passed by it the other day. It looked like they had just about anything you could want. I'll go with you."

My face lights up. "Great! Let me get my keys," I say, already heading back inside.

Ninety minutes later, after pursuing the garden center's endless selections, I purchase three hanging ferns for the porch, two large cobalt-blue ceramic containers for the front steps, and a vibrant assortment of annuals to fill them.

After a quick lunch, we spend the early afternoon hanging the fern baskets and planting the containers. When there's nothing left to do, I can no longer postpone the inevitable. Brushing my hands on my jeans, I run inside to the kitchen for a flashlight and start off across the fields.

"Send in the troops if I'm not back in an hour," I call over my shoulder.

Blossom wastes no time in reaching me, looping her arm through mine. "Oh no, you don't. You're not going in without me."

I smile over at her, not bothering to argue. Truth is, I'm grateful for the company—and her protection. No evil spirits would dare mess with an angel in a cemetery. Right?

Right?

I lead the way through the narrow wooded path, the air thick with damp earth and moss. At the heavy iron gate, I push it open with a creak and step aside, allowing Blossom to enter ahead of me. She wanders among the neat rows of graves, pausing now and then to examine a headstone more closely. Is she talking to someone? And why is she laughing?

While she carries on with her heavenly friends, I focus on my own search, scanning the names and dates etched into the stones. A sudden realization takes my breath. A member of the Malone family has lived in Marsh Hollow for more than four centuries. I can't sell this property. It's more than land and an old farmhouse —it's a legacy. And it's my responsibility to carry it forward.

Inhaling deeply, I make a beeline for the statue, drop to my knees, and press open the hidden panel on the back. I angle my flashlight into the darkened compartment. At first, I see nothing, but then a faint glint catches my eye.

Blossom appears beside me, and I crane my neck to look up at her.

"Here goes." As I slip my hand inside the dark cavern, I squeeze my eyes shut, praying a venomous snake doesn't sink its fangs into my skin. I pat around the moist ground, my fingers brushing against something cold and hard. I reach in with both hands and pull out a small metal box, its surface mottled with rust. A lock sits at the top, and instinct tells me the key in my pocket will fit.

Digging out the key, I insert it into the lock.

Blossom grabs my shoulder. "Wait! Don't you want to open that inside?" Her eyes dart around the cemetery. "What if someone is watching us?"

"If they're watching us here, they'll follow us to the house. Either way, our goose is cooked."

The lock sticks, and I have to wrestle with the key until it finally gives. I creak open the lid and peer inside. Four identical leather-bound journals stare back at me.

I pick up the top one and thumb through the pages. Mama's handwriting fills the lines, chronicling her life beginning in December of 1966.

A chill runs through me. The answers I've been searching for—maybe even the ones I don't want to know—are waiting inside these pages.

Twenty-One

AURELIA'S JOURNAL 1

December 12, 1966

My parents always said I could have my choice of husbands. As long as they are a Dominion First-born, of course. I've had my eye on two young men, nice boys I've known all my life. Then, out of the blue, my parents inform me I'm to marry a man twenty years older than me. *An old man*! My parents are thrilled with the match. Of all the young women, the Society Elder picked me. As if I care. Mama told me to stop crying. She gave me this journal.

Crying won't fix it. But writing might help you understand why it hurts.

You're a woman now, Aurelia. A wife soon. It's time to set aside childish dreams and embrace your duty.

But what if I don't want to embrace it? What if I don't care about duty, or honor, or whatever nonsense they keep feeding me? I want love. I want to choose the man I'm to spend my life with. Is that too much to ask?

March 13, 1967

Everyone has lost their minds. All anyone can talk about is this wedding. *The Marriage of a Century* they're calling it—the season's most beautiful first-born and a powerful US senator. Everett is nice-looking—for an old man. But he's so serious. I've yet to see him crack a smile.

After our fairytale wedding at Briarwood Hall, his family's estate in Middleburg, we'll live in his grand townhome in Georgetown. I've spent my entire life on a farm. What do I know about being a politician's wife? A socialite? Why am I the only one who can see that I'm in over my head?

June 17, 1967

The honeymoon ended the moment Everett carried me over the threshold of our suite at the Ritz in Paris. He ripped off all my clothes and took what he wanted with no compassion and little regard for my virginity. Afterward, he told me with a straight face that he married me for my looks and pedigree. My primary duties are to entertain his guests and bear his children.

My parents have committed me to a lifetime of misery.

June 25, 1967

Everett says the sex will get better with time. But I don't see how—not with the way he gropes, pinches, and squeezes. When I told him he was hurting me, he backhanded me across the face. He's careful, though—never leaving bruises where anyone might see them. Especially not when he insists I wear those skimpy bikinis. I think he secretly enjoys watching other men ogle me.

This isn't a honeymoon. This is a whirlwind tour of the French Riviera, parading me in front of every wealthy businessman, Hollywood stars, and powerful politicians. I sit in silence, sipping champagne, while they discuss things I don't understand and laugh at jokes I don't find funny.

I pray that our life together after the honeymoon will be more meaningful than this.

September 17, 1967

As I feared, my life is nothing more than a carefully curated performance. I am expected to smile, nod, and play the dutiful wife while the men talk politics, and the other wives exchange polished insults about one another's gowns and social standing.

I don't belong here. I can't seem to master the art of idle conversation, nor do I care to. The other wives whisper behind my back, calling me naïve, unsophisticated. Everett tells me to try harder, to watch and learn, to mold myself into the woman they expect me to be.

But no matter how many dinner parties I attend, draped in the latest couture, I remain an outsider—a country girl playing pretend in a world that will never truly accept me.

Even Everett's very large staff of servants know I don't belong. They watch me with quiet pity, exchanging glances when I fumble over the simplest tasks expected of a senator's wife. The housekeeper hides a smirk when I struggle to remember the name of yet another ambassador's wife. The butler, ever professional, avoids my gaze entirely, as if pretending I don't exist.

I wonder if they place bets on how long I'll last.

The other morning, I heard the maids whispering in the upstairs hall outside our bedroom. Several years ago, Everett's first wife, Belinda—which he neglected to tell me about prior to the wedding—drowned in their swimming pool at Briarwood Hall. They don't think it was an accident. One maid swore she saw bruises on Belinda's arms weeks before her death. Another claims she heard a heated argument between them the night before she drowned.

Apparently, his wife was unable to conceive, and Everett is desperate for children, offspring to carry on the Meyer legacy. A wife who can't provide him with heirs has no value. God forbid that happens to me. We've only been married for three months. Surely, he doesn't expect a miracle. I should be terrified. Maybe I am. But mostly, I feel trapped.

December 12, 1967

Instead of lifting my spirits, the endless whirl of Christmas parties drains me. I count down the days until we leave for Briarwood Hall. I hope the crisp country air might shake me from this fog—though I doubt it. With any luck, Everett will be too busy shooting birds to pay much attention to me. But he watches me closely, like a hawk, for signs that I might be pregnant. Whenever the Kotex pads appear in the bathroom, his mood turns stormy, his temper barely contained. I've grown exhausted by his brooding silences, his sharp words, and the way he shoves me when no one is looking—always careful never to leave a mark.

December 27, 1967

I wasn't prepared for how much I would miss my parents at Christmas. I should've thought to invite them to Briarwood Hall, though I doubt Everett would've allowed it. He can barely hide how little he thinks of them, as though they aren't good enough for the mighty Meyer family. When I remind him my ancestor was the founding elder, he waves it off.

That was a long time ago. The Malone family has been unremarkable ever since.

I wish I had the courage to ask him why he married me if I don't meet his high standards.

Desperate to escape, I asked for permission to visit my family for New Year's. Everett refused without hesitation. He says we need to focus on his re-election campaign, that my place is by his side. As if I have a choice. Political rallies will now fill my already packed social calendar, ensuring I never have a moment to myself.

January 20, 1968

I begged Everett to help me find my purpose. If I can't be a good wife in his eyes, maybe I can be something else, something of value. I asked him to send me to college, to let me study, to become a teacher, an accountant, a nurse—anything to fill my days with more than empty parties and polite conversation. I even offered to help with his campaign, thinking maybe I could make myself useful as his manager. He laughed in my face.

Your only purpose as my wife is to smile pretty for the cameras and give me a child.

When I suggested I resume training with Mama to be a midwife, his face twisted with disgust, and his fist slammed against the dining table so hard the silver rattled. *Absolutely not! You are married to a United States senator. Being a midwife is beneath you.*

When I argued Mama was the society's premier midwife, a woman revered for her skills, a role she had dedicated her life to, he mimicked me in a high-pitched singsong voice. *Mama is a midwife.*

Then, suddenly, his hand was in my hair, twisting painfully at the roots as he yanked me toward him.

Your mother performs a very important duty. But that duty is not for you. You are destined for greater things. You are destined to be the mother of my children.

That is all I am to him. A vessel. A means to an end. Nothing more.

March 13, 1968

The dreary winter weather refuses to lift, and neither does my mood. Even a weekend at Briarwood Hall hasn't helped. I'm desperate to get pregnant—not just to appease Everett, but for myself. I long for a baby to dote on, to love and cuddle, to dress in sweet little clothes. A pregnancy would also be my escape, the perfect excuse to decline the party invitations that arrive by the dozens every week.

July 20, 1968

After much begging and pleading, Everett has finally agreed to let me visit my parents for two weeks. I burst into tears the moment I saw Mama and Papa, and I haven't stopped crying since. I told them everything—how miserable my life is, how Everett mistreats me, and how I don't belong in Washington society.

Mama, in so many words, told me to grow up and accept my reality. Papa ordered me to get a hold of myself—*No man wants a wife who cries all the time.* When I mentioned Everett's first wife—her inability to conceive and her mysterious death —they barely reacted.

I had hoped Papa might pull Everett aside when he arrived to take me home, that he might say something, anything, about the way he treats me. But he said nothing. Not one single word.

I am on my own. If I don't get pregnant soon, I may find myself floating at the bottom of a swimming pool.

August 21, 1968

We are spending two weeks at Briarwood Hall while the senate is on break. Most days—and many evenings—Everett is away at campaign events. Fortunately, he only expects me to attend the most important ones with him. He wants me to learn tennis and horseback riding. Tennis, I enjoy. An instructor from Everett's club drives out to Briarwood Hall three times a week for my lessons. But horses, I can do without. The massive creatures terrify me almost as much as his grumpy old trainer.

A few nights ago, just after midnight, I had ventured downstairs to the kitchen for a glass of milk when I overheard hushed voices coming from Everett's study. I crept down the hall and pressed my ear to the door. They spoke so softly I could only catch fragments of the conversation, but I clearly heard the words *Klan* and *Jeremiah Whitaker*.

This morning when I opened the paper, I was stunned to see the front-page story reporting that a prominent civil rights lawyer and advocate had been murdered in his home the night before. Authorities suspect involvement by the Ku Klux Klan.

The man's name was Jeremiah Whitaker.

September 3, 1968

Sadly, our time at Briarwood Hall has ended. Tomorrow, we'll return to Washington for the final months of Everett's re-election campaign. My head spins at the endless parties and events I'm expected to attend. But soon, it will be all over.

Secretly, I hope he loses so we can return to Briarwood for good.

I've been paying closer attention to the many business associates who visit my husband at home. Some are working on his campaign. Others are longtime associates from the Dominion Society, most of whom I already know. But the rest —shady-looking characters with hard eyes and whispered conversations—are not the sort of men my husband usually entertains.

I've started keeping a record in the blank ledger I found in Everett's bottom desk drawer. Every name. Every hushed meeting. Every whispered detail that seems off. I've also begun paying closer attention to the news. I have a growing suspicion my husband is involved in something nefarious.

Does he belong to the Ku Klux Klan?

Is he capable of having a man murdered?

Did he order a hit on his own wife?

Twenty-Two

2008

I stay up late reading on Tuesday night. As much as I'm dying of curiosity, I don't rush through Mama's journals. I savor each word, letting the reality of her world settle over me. An arranged marriage? Never in a million years would I have imagined Mama as a senator's wife. She told me so little about my father, only that he had died in a tragic car accident when I was a baby. I never even knew his name. Until now.

Everett.

The name sends a cold ripple through me. The same name Mama whispered—argued with—late at night in her bedroom. The voice that answered her in the dark.

When I go down for breakfast on Wednesday morning, I'm grateful Blossom doesn't press for details. She knows I will tell her everything in time.

I drain the last of my coffee and set my mug down. "I decided to finish painting the house and redo my bedroom."

Blossom beams. "I'll help."

I push back from the table, smiling. "I was hoping you'd say that. I'm going to town for supplies. Wanna come?"

"You bet! Let me grab my purse."

On the drive to Colton, I fill Blossom in on Mama's first months of marriage—her aversion to the endless social obligations of a politician's wife, his mistreatment of her, and her growing suspicions about my father's underhanded dealings.

"Everett Meyer was a powerful man, and the Dominion Society was more than a social club. The leaders—referred to as the Elders—were corrupt. Some may even have been tied to the Ku Klux Klan."

Blossom clucks her tongue. "Good heavens. That explains why Dominion is still so secretive. Once you go that deep into the darkness, there's no coming back."

I swallow hard. "That's what's worrying me. I'm just beginning to learn about my father, but I have a sick feeling I won't like what I find out." I slip into an empty parking space in front of a row of shops on Main Street. "But for now, let's forget about Mama and her diaries and focus on redoing my bedroom."

At a linens boutique, I purchase an oatmeal-colored matelassé comforter and matching European shams and decorative pillows in cheerful stripes of pink, blue, and yellow. Next door, at an interiors store, I find a natural jute rug woven with a subtle diamond pattern, the perfect finishing touch.

"What color will you paint the walls?" Blossom asks as we head to the hardware store.

I smile over at her. "I love the pale oak color you chose for downstairs. I'm thinking of extending it up the stairs, down the hallway, and into my bedroom."

Blossom nods approvingly. "Excellent choice. You can't beat it for a whole-house color."

Back at home, we strip the old comforter off my bed and roll up the worn shag carpet, hauling both outside to the dumpster.

"I gather your sister hasn't returned your call," Blossom

says as we drag the furniture to the center of the room in preparation for painting.

I shake my head. "Nope. She's avoiding me."

Blossom straightens, pressing a hand to her lower back. "I wouldn't assume that."

"She is. And honestly? I'm not in a hurry to talk to her anyway. I'm furious she kept Mama's journals from me."

Blossom tilts her head. "Maybe she had a good reason, Goldie. Maybe she was protecting you from something in them."

I frown. "I hadn't thought of that. You might be right. I'll try her again later."

But I'm suddenly more eager than ever to talk to my sister. When Blossom goes to the kitchen to make lunch, I slip outside to the porch, phone in hand. My heart pounds as I tap in the number.

When the receptionist answers, I ask for Melanie Stone and give my name. She lets out an exaggerated sigh. "Geez, lady. Can't you take a hint? Your sister doesn't want to talk to you."

I grip the phone harder. "I don't care what she wants. I'm her sister, and I need to speak with her."

"Is it a matter of life or death?" she snaps.

Yes, it's a matter of death—but not the way she means. "Not exactly."

"Then don't call back." Click.

I stare at the phone, bewildered. Why won't she speak to me? I consider trying to reach out to Gunner, but I'm not that desperate yet.

———

With the transformation underway, the house—its creaking floors, sunlit rooms, and quiet whispers of the past—feels less like a relic of my childhood and more like a part of me. And I find myself seriously contemplating moving to Marsh Hollow permanently.

For two days, Blossom and I work tirelessly, painting my bedroom and the upstairs hallway, breathing new life into the space. Moving downstairs, we scrub the alcove paneling with Murphys Oil Soap until the cypress gleams, then strip away the faded, burgundy-striped wallpaper from the dining room walls.

The kitchen requires the most work. It takes several coats of pale robin's-egg blue—three shades lighter than the cabinets —to cover the dreadful *DV* graffiti. But once the project is complete, with its red Formica countertops and vintage charm, the kitchen takes on a true retro vibe.

As I work, I mentally arrange my furniture from Richmond. My small walnut desk is the perfect size for the alcove. And in the dining room, I'm thinking of putting my pine farm table in front of the window, with my cozy club chairs tucked into the corner.

I get carried away as I envision bigger changes. Blowing out the wall between the kitchen and the dining room, replacing it with a breakfast counter. Painting is only a temporary facelift. Eventually I'll need new cabinets and updated appliances. Why not renovate the bathrooms while I'm at it? The proceeds from selling my townhouse will more than cover it.

I chuckle to myself. These projects will keep Sam busy for a while, and I certainly enjoy having him around.

Speaking of Sam, I haven't heard from him all week. I tell myself he's busy with his new project, but a small part of me worries I've offended him. So when he calls late Thursday afternoon, inviting me for dinner Saturday night, relief, tinged with excitement, rushes over me.

"Are you going to read more of your mama's diary tonight?" Blossom asks me over dinner.

We're eating mixed green salads with grilled shrimp at the picnic table on the porch. The overhead fan stirs the mild evening air, offering relief from the lingering warmth of the setting sun.

"I'm going to try. I was too tired from all the physical labor to read any last night." I pop a shrimp into my mouth. "When I finish with them, I'll hand the diaries over to you."

Blossom looks at me over a forkful of salad. "Are you sure? Those are your mama's most intimate thoughts. I wouldn't want to intrude."

"I trust you, Blossom, and I want you to read them." I wink, mischief tugging at my lips. "I'm going to tell you everything anyway."

Blossom's smile is warm, her green eyes soft with understanding. "In that case, I'd be honored."

Twenty-Three

September 28, 1968

Everett was furious when I got my period. This time, he didn't just sulk—he threatened me. Actually, threatened me. *Either get pregnant, or else.*

Angry and afraid, I confronted him. *Or else what? You'll drown me in the pool like Belinda.*

He didn't deny it. The silence was worse than any confirmation.

I suggested we might have better luck conceiving if he treated me with some respect in bed—if he slowed down instead of being so rushed and clumsy. His clenched jaw told me I'd hit a nerve, and the next time we had sex was different. *He* was different. Almost even tender.

Now I wait. If I'm right, if it worked, wouldn't that be something?

November 28, 1968

Everett won his re-election by a landslide. He's so thrilled, I can't help but be pleased for him. As a delayed celebration, he's invited a large group for Thanksgiving dinner at Briarwood. I'll wait until this evening, after the guests have gone to share my big news.

The doctor confirmed it yesterday—I'm finally pregnant.

For once, I don't mind being surrounded by people I barely know or women who despise me for reasons I don't understand.

Maybe now I'll get some peace.

Maybe even a little respect.

January 11, 1969

Pregnancy agrees with me. I only attend the parties I choose—almost none—and Everett doesn't lay a finger on me for fear of harming his beloved child. He's convinced it's a boy. I'm certain it's a girl. He claims he'll be happy either way, but if it's a daughter, we'll be trying again soon for a son.

April 12, 1969

I am deeply disturbed by the things I hear late at night with my ear pressed to the study door, both at Briarwood and in Washington. Days later, the names mentioned appear in the papers, attached to unexplained disappearances or tragic accidents. The connection is impossible to ignore.

Mama came to visit this week, helping me shop for the baby. This afternoon, as we sat on a park bench at the Tidal Basin, admiring the late-blooming cherry blossoms, I mentioned Everett's extracurricular activities.

She warned me to stop my spying at once. *What you're doing is dangerous, Aurelia.*

Then, for the first time, she spoke of our family's ties to the Dominion Society. My ancestor, Ambrose Malone, was its founding member. His intent had been honorable—to form a network of families who had arrived from England together, supporting one another and strengthening their bloodlines. But corruption seeped in, as it always does. My ancestors distanced themselves as best they could from the society's darker dealings. But the women in our family had no choice. They were bound to the role of premier midwife, a duty passed down through generations. Had I not married Everett, that responsibility would have fallen to me.

Mama claims that members of today's Dominion Society are mostly normal families. But we have to be careful of the Elders—the five men who control everything—and the Watchmen, their loyal enforcers who handle the dirty work.

When I asked why they forced me to marry such a ruthless man, Mama's answer shocked me: We didn't choose him, Aurelia. He chose you. And once Everett Meyer sets his sights on something, there's no refusing him—not without consequences.

My parents had no choice but to go along with the arrangement, too afraid of what might happen if they denied him.

I asked Mama why we didn't just withdraw from the society. Her response chilled me to the bone.

Once a member, always a member. Death is the only way out.

July 26, 1969

I don't know what to make of tonight's events. A man just died in my house?

I was pacing in the upstairs hallway, unable to sleep with the baby pressing on my bladder, when a commotion in the foyer below caught my attention. Crouching low beneath the chair railing, I watched in horror as Reginald Thorne and Victor Aldridge dragged a black man into the house, leaving a dark trail in their wake. I gasped and quickly covered my mouth, praying they hadn't heard me. But they were too preoccupied, speaking in hushed but urgent tones as they stripped the man's torn clothing away.

When they flipped him over, my stomach lurched, and I thought I might vomit.

Crisscrossing his back were raw, bloody welts.

For a fleeting minute, I clung to the desperate hope that they had brought him here to rescue him. That they were trying to save him. But then I heard Victor announce he was dead. And Reginald kicked the man hard in the side. *Get him out of here.*

Tears streamed down my face as I slipped back into bed, my body trembling beneath the sheets. When Everett finally crawled in hours later, I kept my eyes shut and my breathing even. I couldn't bear to look at him. I'm married to a murderer. And the child growing inside me carries his blood.

I've yet to learn the name of the poor man they beat to death. His story never appeared in the papers. Perhaps he wasn't important enough.

August 9, 1969

The baby arrived early and fast, too fast for Mama to get here in time to deliver her. And so, Melanie Malone Meyer

153

became the first baby in our family's long history to be born in a hospital.

Everett seemed unbothered. *These things can't be helped.*

Mama arrived an hour later, frazzled from her journey but overjoyed to meet her grandchild. Everett immediately ordered the hospital staff out of the room, allowing Mama to perform the midwife rituals that had been passed down through the generations—the whispered Latin oath, the inked seal pressed onto Melanie's tiny heel, the delicate silver thread tied around her wrist, binding her to the ancestors who came before her. Symbolic gestures, but ones that carried the weight of tradition.

Mama will stay with me for a few days, not as a midwife but as my mother. And for that, I am grateful. I'm not worried about taking care of my newborn. After what I've seen these past few weeks—things I don't dare put into words—I'm terrified to be alone with my husband.

October 3, 1969

Being a mother hasn't granted me approval into the Washington Political Wives Club as I'd hoped. In fact, my invitations to their tedious gatherings have dwindled. I suspect these insufferable women are jealous—of my husband's influence and my daughter's beauty.

Feigning the baby blues, I have retreated to Briarwood Hall, where the crisp autumn air and fiery foliage instantly lifted my spirits. Melanie thrives here, her rosy cheeks proof of the fresh country air. Each day, I stroll her for hours—across the sprawling estate, down the tree-lined drive, and along the charming streets of town. The staff understands I dislike being fussed over, and I've made it clear that I can manage just fine on my own. I promote one of the maids—a natural with infants—to nanny and return to my tennis lessons, reclaiming a bit of myself.

December 20, 1969

My improved mood was short-lived. My heart overflows with love for my child, and watching her blossom brings me great joy. But the solitude at Briarwood Hall is wearing on me. I have an honest-to-goodness case of the baby blues—or maybe it's something more. It feels heavier. Like depression.

The young women Everett has introduced me to, all from respectable families who belong to his hunt club, are certainly kinder than the politicians' wives, but they're obsessed with horses, and I have little in common with them. When I suggested inviting my parents for Christmas, he immediately shut me down.

We have our own family now, Aurelia. I'm looking forward to spending Melanie's first Christmas—just the three of us.

His words were meant to be reassuring. Instead, they left me feeling lonelier than ever.

February 6, 1970

More snow is in the forecast for the weekend. I think I'll lose what's left of my mind if I have to watch another flake drift from the sky, piling onto the endless white expanse that already smothers Briarwood Hall. The cold seeps into everything—into my bones, into my mood, into the hollow spaces of this house.

And to make matters worse, Everett is due home at any moment. His desire for a son has grown into an obsession, a constant undercurrent in our conversations, a silent expectation that weighs on me. At some point this weekend, I'll have to tell him. My period arrived this morning, sealing another month of failure. Another month of trying, wasted.

Everett is proud of Melanie—his firstborn, his daughter—but only in the abstract. She will have the finest education, a grand debutante season, and an advantageous marriage. He has ensured her future is secured, yet he barely acknowledges her in the present. She's four months old, and he hasn't held her once.

Sometimes, I wonder if he's capable of love at all. Apparently not for her. Definitely not for me.

February 20, 1970

Late-night visits from Everett's friends and associates have become alarmingly more frequent. Reginald and Victor are always around whenever Everett is in residence, their presence as constant and ominous as the shadows lurking in the corners of this house.

When it's only two of them, I sneak downstairs to listen. But when more arrive, I don't dare leave my bedroom for fear of being seen. Instead, I watch from my window, tracking their movements, recording the makes of cars and license plate numbers in my ledger.

Through the air ducts, I hear their murmured conversations—not the words, just the significance of them. The urgency. The unmistakable tension in their voices.

A sinking feeling takes hold, settling in my bones. They're planning something. Something big. Something dangerous.

February 23, 1970

The sound of car doors slamming in the courtyard below woke me just after midnight. Peeking through the window, I caught glimpses of Reginald, Victor, and several other Dominion members slipping into the house.

I couldn't help myself. I had to know what was happening.

I crept down the back stairs into the living room, pressing my ear against the wall outside Everett's study. Their hushed voices carried through the wood—low, urgent, deliberate.

They were discussing Virginia Senator Raymond Alden, a longtime ally who had suddenly become a liability. He is threatening to go public with everything—election rigging, financial corruption, the criminal enterprise they secretly control. Alden knows it all. And he's blackmailing them, threatening to blow the whistle to the press.

The decision was swift. They can't let him talk.

Everett gave the order, his voice chillingly calm. The others murmured their agreement.

They left suddenly, too suddenly. I didn't have time to slip back upstairs unnoticed. As I tiptoed toward the staircase, I nearly collided with Everett.

I stammered out an excuse about getting a glass of milk. But there was no glass in my hand. He knew I was lying.

He didn't press me. He only watched me, his gaze unreadable, as though debating whether I was worth the trouble. Then, with an air of exhaustion, he walked me back to our room and tucked me into bed.

Leaning in close, his breath hot against my cheek, he whispered in my ear. *You might see and hear things in this house you don't understand. But it's best if you forget about them. I'm a powerful man in this state. Sometimes, I have to make tough decisions for the right reason.*

His voice dropped lower. *And if I find out you told*

anybody about this, I'll beat you senseless. I don't care if you are the mother of my child.

I didn't sleep after that.

At dawn, I went downstairs for coffee. From the cook's small television in the corner came the morning news—Senator Raymond Alden had died in a tragic accident. Hit by a city bus while walking to his office on Capitol Hill. The official story appears airtight. But I know the truth. And the names are in my ledger.

Twenty-Four

2008

I slide Mama's first two diaries across the table to Blossom at breakfast on Friday morning. "In reading her words, I feel like I'm watching my mother grow up—from an unsophisticated farm girl to a young woman finding her place in the world. She might not have been the wife Everett wanted, but she was becoming her own person, and I find myself rooting for her."

Blossom opens the diary and gently fans the pages. "Thank you for trusting me enough to read them."

I shake my head. "I should thank *you*. I *need* you to read them—to help me sort through everything I'm feeling."

Blossom's expression turns thoughtful. "What sort of feelings, Goldie?"

"There all mixed up." I sit back in my chair, coffee mug in hand. "My father was a powerful man. And extremely dangerous. I hate him for the way he treated Mama. He barely tolerated Mellie. He was desperate for a son. I can only imagine how devastated he was when I was born."

I pause to sip my coffee.

"The more I learn about Mama, the more I soften toward her." A smile tugs at my lips, my gaze distant. "She loved

159

playing tennis. Can you believe that? I can't imagine Mama dressed in tennis whites, swinging a racquet." My smile fades. "I feel sorry for her though. She was so lonely. Ostracized by the other politician's wives. Treated with such disrespect by her husband."

My mind drifts back to the diary entries I read last night. "Mama talks a lot about her mother, my grandmother, a woman I never knew."

Blossom grins. "Well now, that's special."

I smile. "Very much so. As a child, I never thought much about midwifery. To me, it was just Mama's job—something that took her away for long stretches but that kept food on our table. By the time I realized most women have their babies in hospitals, I had already left home. For most of my adult life, I saw midwifery as primitive, outdated. But for some, it was something else entirely—a sacred ritual—an intimate moment shared between the birth mother and the midwife. Knowing Mama played that role in countless deliveries makes me incredibly proud of her. And all the Malone women before her."

My eyes travel to the wall where the *DV* seal once loomed. "She talks about the Dominion Society. The intruders who broke in here were likely Watchmen, the thugs who carry out criminal activity for the Elders—the leaders of the society. Dominion was intended to be a honorable institution. The founding families came from England together, bound by loyalty. Their goal was to stay connected, support one another, and strengthen their bloodlines through marriage. But corruption crept in, twisting their legacy. My mother's parents tried to distance themselves from it as best they could."

I exhale slowly, my chest aching. "My father, on the other hand, epitomized the worst of it." I shiver as a chill slides down my spine. "And to think his blood runs through my veins."

Sam surprises me with a trip to Colton for dinner. Driftwood is a charming, converted farmhouse near the heart of downtown, its upscale rustic interior blending reclaimed wood, warm candlelight, and exposed brick.

The hostess greets Sam by name and leads us to a secluded table in the corner of the back patio, nestled among large evergreen plants—towering fiddle-leaf figs, fragrant jasmine, and glossy magnolias swaying in the evening breeze.

"I'm impressed," I say to Sam once we've been seated. "I didn't know Colton offered such elegant dining."

"Driftwood has the best food for miles. Getting a reservation is next to impossible. Lucky for me, I know the owner. I renovated this place," Sam says, his chest puffed with pride as he sweeps an arm across the dining area.

I chuckle. "You did a splendid job."

Unfortunately, the service is slow, and we wait thirty minutes for our cocktails.

Tina, the harried waitress, finally arrives with our drinks and an apologetic smile. "Sorry for the wait. We're short-staffed tonight. If you know anyone looking for a job, send them our way."

The words leave my mouth before I can stop them. "Actually, I may be looking soon."

Tina perks up. "Really? Do you have any waitressing experience?"

"Twenty-plus years at the same Italian restaurant in Richmond," I tell her.

Her face lights up. "That works."

I lean in slightly, lowering my voice. "What's it like working here? Are the tips good?"

"You bet. We're the only upscale restaurant around. Our regulars tip well, and we're only open for dinner four nights a week—Wednesday through Saturday." She pauses, hopeful. "Do you want me to grab the manager?"

I hesitate. "I'm not ready to commit just yet. I'm still figuring out my living situation."

"I get it." Tina nods and moves on to another table.

I turn back to Sam, who's grinning from ear to ear.

I tilt my head. "What're you smiling at?"

His smile lingers. "Sounds to me like someone is thinking of making a permanent move to Marsh Hollow."

"I'm considering my options," I say in a clipped tone.

Mischief glints in his eyes. "Once you sample the food, you'll be begging for a job here."

I wag my finger at him. "Ah-ha. You had an ulterior motive for bringing here."

Sam shrugs. "Maybe."

But Sam is right. Dinner is outstanding—thick-cut, bone-in ribeyes; truffle parmesan fries; and charred asparagus with lemon zest. For dessert, we share a dark chocolate tart with a sea salt caramel drizzle and a dollop of fresh whipped cream.

As Sam is signing the credit card receipt, Tina slips me the restaurant's business card with a name and number scrawled on the back.

"I mentioned you to the owner." She taps the card. "That's him—Calvin Drake. He said to call if you're inter-ested in the job. Anytime. All hours are business hours for Calvin. When we're closed, he's either cleaning, restocking, or experimenting with new dishes."

I tuck the card into my purse. "I wouldn't be able to start for a couple of weeks, maybe longer."

Tina leans in, lowering her voice as if sharing a secret. "We're borderline desperate. We'll take you whenever we can get you."

I laugh softly. "Gosh, thanks. It's nice to be wanted."

I'm quiet on the drive home, my mind preoccupied with

thoughts of working at Driftwood. Four nights a week isn't bad, but working weekends would mean barely seeing Sam.

Back at home, I invite him in, and we make out like teenagers on the living room sofa, all thoughts of work pushed aside.

"I'd forgotten how much fun kissing can be," I say, slightly breathless.

"No kidding." Sam laughs and then grows serious. "I'm worried about the next steps though. The things that happen after kissing. I don't want to disappoint you."

"If anything, I'll be the one disappointing *you*." I toy with a loose thread on my blouse. "You were married. I've only been with one man—a boy, really—and only for a brief time."

"I'm fascinated by this boy who stole your heart. Tell me more."

I pull away, straightening my clothes with shaky hands. "Okay. But I need some air. Let's go outside to the porch."

Once we're comfortable in the rockers, the words spill out of me as I stare up at the half-moon. I tell him about my teenage affair with Gunner, my sister running off with him, and the baby that resulted from our brief relationship. When I'm finished, I'm surprised to find my cheeks wet with tears.

Sam squeezes my hand, his touch warm and steady. "I can't imagine how difficult it was for you—discovering you were pregnant and having no one to turn to for help. Raising your son on your own is admirable. You two must be close."

I press my lips thin, my heart aching. I wish that were true. But I'm not ready to admit the truth about my relationship with Nate. "Not as close as I'd like," I murmur in a voice so low Sam doesn't hear me.

Sam studies me for a long moment, then exhales. "You said you feel you need your sister's approval before deciding what to do with the farm. Forgive me, but you don't owe her anything—not when it comes to this place. She ran off with your boyfriend, never contacted you, never visited your mother. And now she's disclaimed her inheritance. Short of giving you the middle finger, I don't know how much clearer she could be. You don't need her permission. She certainly didn't ask for yours when she stole your boyfriend."

"I know you're right, Sam. In my head, it all makes sense. But my heart . . . that's a different matter."

Sam brushes a strand of hair from my face. "You're coping with a lot right now, Lydia. I'd like to be here for you—if you'll let me."

I bite down on my lower lip. "Trust doesn't come easy for me, Sam. But I'd like to try."

He hesitates, then clears his throat. "As far as the . . . you know." His face flushes.

I arch a brow. "Sex?"

He smiles a little sheepishly. "Yeah. Sex." His voice softens. "That you've only been with one man . . . It makes you special, Lydia. And me? I consider myself a lucky guy. We'll take it slow. We won't do anything until we're both ready."

"Even if it means waiting until Christmas?"

He nods. "Even then. I just hope you're still here at Christmas."

His words comfort me like a warm blanket. But I'm not sure I can give him the answer he wants.

Twenty-Five

Sunday morning I hang my paintings and sketches with clothespins to fishing line strung around my studio. My thoughts are all over the place—on Sam, on Aurelia, on my father and all the destruction he left behind. As far as Mellie is concerned, Sam is right. I don't need her approval. I've tried contacting her, but she obviously doesn't want to be reached. I owe her nothing.

I wait until after lunch to call Calvin Drake, the restaurant owner. His talk of fine cuisine and superior service warms my heart, reminding me of my dear friends, Giorgio and Carmela. I share my work history, promising to send my résumé along with Carmela's recommendation letter.

I'm surprised when Drake hires me on the spot. "It's difficult to find good help these days. And you have just the qualifications I'm looking for."

I accept without hesitation, which feels like a sign—maybe I'm more ready to make the move to Marsh Hollow than I thought.

I explain that I've inherited my family home and need a little more time to get settled before starting work.

"I understand," he says. "But I'll need you no later than June first. Business picks up dramatically in the summers."

"June first works for me," I say. "I may even be able to start sooner. I'll be in touch as soon as I have a better handle on my schedule."

We talk a minute longer before ending the call.

Next, I call Brandy, who answers with a cheerful hello. "I was going to call you today. Guess what? I got a job at Mamma Zu. It's a great place to work, and they're teaching me to bartend."

The excitement in her voice brings a smile to my face. "Good for you! Congratulations."

"Are you ready for the best part?" She barely pauses before babbling on. "One of the waitresses is looking for a roommate. I'm moving in with her at the end of the month. You'll have your house back to yourself when you come home."

I cough, clearing my throat. "That's actually why I'm calling. I'm not coming back to Richmond. I've accepted a new job, and I'm moving to Marsh Hollow for good."

Brandy lets out a squeal. "What? That's wonderful, Lydia. You go, girl!"

"Thanks. I'm excited. It's a good thing you found a roommate, since I'll be putting the townhouse on the market soon."

"Now you won't have to kick me out," she giggles. "Oh! Before I forget," she says, with a shift in tone. "Your son came by the other day looking for you. He's been trying to reach you. He's worried about you, Lydia."

My heart skips a beat. Nate is trying to reach me. "The cell service here is awful."

"I'm sure it's nothing, but . . ." Her voice trails off.

"But what, Brandy?"

She hesitates. "While your son was here, he asked for a drink of water. It was a scorcher, and he'd been riding his bike. I went into the kitchen to grab one for him. When I came back

. . . I caught him flipping through a stack of your mail. I've been meaning to send it to you, by the way."

Why was Nate going through my mail?

"Don't worry about the mail. I'll be coming to Richmond soon to start prepping for the move."

"Okay. Just let me know when, and I'll make sure the house is spotless. Anyway, after your son left, I noticed the letter from your attorney was missing. I'm not saying he took it, but I've looked everywhere for it, and I can't find it."

Letter from my attorney?

Then I remember—Marge mentioned they'd sent the probate authorization forms to my Richmond address.

I take a slow breath. "It's fine, Brandy. The attorney's office brought over duplicate copies."

"Whew! I was worried it was something important. I gotta run now, Lydia. We'll talk soon," Brandy says and ends the call.

I'm still staring at my phone when Blossom emerges from the house with a tray of sweet tea and pound cake. She sets the tray on the small table and eases into the chair beside her. "What's the matter, Goldie Girl? You're off on another planet."

"Nothing's wrong. I'm trying to decide whether to clear out my house before putting it on the market. Or whether it will sell better with the furniture in it."

"Woo-hoo! You've decided to stay!" She offers me a high five. "That's excellent news, Goldie Girl."

I smile. "Thanks. I'm excited. At least part of me is. The other part is wondering what I'm doing." I drop my phone into my lap and lean my head back against the chair. "I've renovated the house and accepted a job. Why am I still having reservations about making this move?"

Blossom studies me for a moment, then leans forward. "It's a big change, Goldie. Having second thoughts is natural."

I exhale slowly, staring at the ceiling. "It still feels . . . unsettled."

She nods. "Because change doesn't feel like certainty. It feels like standing on the edge of something unknown. But that doesn't mean it's wrong. It just means you're stepping into a new chapter." She reaches over and squeezes my hand. "You don't have to be fearless, Lydia. You just have to be willing."

I smile softly. "I'm willing. I think."

Her eyes shimmer with something deeper than joy. "This place may be full of shadows, but it's also full of light. And I reckon God brought you back here for a reason. Marsh Hollow's not just where you come from. It's where you're meant to grow. You don't have to run from the past anymore, sugar. You've just got to stand in it, claim it, and let the good Lord work the rest out."

Her words hit me deep, stirring something tender and raw. My throat burns, and for a moment, I don't trust my voice to speak.

"As for the furniture, sounds like a question for your Realtor," she says with a chuckle.

"First, I need to hire a Realtor."

"That should be easy enough," Blossom says. "Which of your furniture will you move down here?"

"There's not room for much. I'll bring my mahogany poster bed down from Richmond. A pair of chairs and my pine table for the dining room. I have no clue what to do with the rest."

Blossom sips her tea. "Can your son use any of it?"

"Not in his current apartment. And our tastes are very different." I tap my chin, thinking. "I could store some things in the barn. At least until he gets married. But that's a long way off."

Blossom snaps her fingers. "Problem solved. Will you call him back?"

I sit up straight, my head swiveling toward her. "How did you know he's tried to reach me? Were you eavesdropping while I was on the phone?"

"Eavesdropping?" Blossom places a hand over her heart, feigning innocence. "You should know me better than that by now."

I laugh, settling back into my chair. "Right. I forgot. You just know these things." I pick up my phone and put it back down. "I'm too tired today. I'll call him tomorrow."

Blossom pinches off a bite of pound cake, pops it into her mouth, and licks her fingers. "And your sister?"

"What about her? I've tried calling. She doesn't want to talk to me."

Blossom lets out a humph. "If you say so."

I glare at her, irritation prickling my skin. "What do you expect me to do, Blossom? Fly to New York and barge into her office?"

She purses her lips, considering. "That could work. What I don't expect is for you to give up."

I sigh, my frustration deflating. "I'm grateful for all you've done for me, Blossom. I never would have survived these past few weeks without you. But I'm feeling stronger every day, and I can take it from here. I'm sure you have other lost souls to save."

"You're not getting rid of me that easily. Besides, I'm not convinced your soul is at peace yet." She reaches into the deep pocket of her dress and sets Mama's diaries on the table between us. "Here's the thing about new chapters. You don't get to pick and choose which parts you carry forward. You have to turn the page, even when the words make you ache." Her voice softens. "Sometimes, the hardest stories to face are the ones that still need an ending."

169

Twenty-Six

AMELIA'S JOURNAL 3

May 13, 1970

Everett is determined to make a fox hunter out of me. Last week, when I admitted I'm afraid of his horse trainer, he chuckled and confessed that he, too, had once feared the old man. Then, out of the blue, he fired him and hired a young trainer from Kentucky, who is due to arrive next week.

Now I have no excuse not to try riding.

May 20, 1970

Whit Calloway is not what I expected—a breath of fresh air after the crass old trainer. He's surprisingly young, not much older than me, with golden hair and striking blue-green eyes. He's tall and muscular, built for handling large animals, but there's a quiet gentleness about him that offers reassurance.

For my first lesson, instead of tossing me into the saddle, he took a different approach. He walked me through the horse breeds and their colorings, then showed me how to properly groom them. I found the exercise calming—the rhythmic brushstrokes and the warmth of the animal beneath my hands.

By my second lesson, we were already riding the trails that wind through Briarwood. We stopped at a stream where, to my surprise, he'd arranged a picnic with the staff—a thoughtful gesture that caught me off guard.

Getting to know my students helps me be a more responsive and effective teacher, he explained.

We sat by the water for over an hour while the horses grazed nearby. Whit is easy to talk to, his smile softening into dimples that light up his face.

For the first time since marrying Everett, I feel like I've made a friend.

June 14, 1970

Whit is a gifted instructor, and I've taken to riding surprisingly well, considering my initial hesitation. He says I have a natural seat. Seat! I'm learning all the horse lingo now. My posture is improving, my hands steadier on the reins. I've mastered trotting and cantering, and next up is jumping. The thought sends a thrill through me, a mixture of nerves and excitement.

Of all the horses in the stable, Magnolia suits me best. She's a graceful, dapple gray mare with a smooth gait and a patient temperament—perfect for a rider still finding her confidence. She challenges me just enough, sensing when I need a nudge forward but never overwhelming me. Whit says she's intuitive, the kind of horse that reads her rider's emotions and adjusts accordingly. I trust her, and that trust makes all the difference.

Melanie has fallen head over heels for Whit. She squeals with delight whenever he scoops her up and spins her around, her little hands clutching his shirt like she never wants to let go. The other day, he even took her on her first horseback ride, perched in the saddle in front of him as they trotted around the ring. She giggled the entire time, completely enchanted.

Watching them together, I feel something stir in my chest. Not quite longing, not quite regret. Just the ache of knowing that moments like these, fleeting as they are, can feel more like home than the house I married into.

July 24, 1970

I look forward to my daily riding lesson more than I should. It's become the highlight of my day, the one place I feel truly free. But it's not just the riding. It's Whit.

At night, when I'm alone in bed, I think of him. Improper things. The way his shirt clings to him when he wipes the sweat from his brow. The warmth of his hands on my waist as he steadies me in the saddle. His touch lingers just a second too long—and I don't pull away.

I know he feels it too. I see it in the way his gaze lingers when he thinks I'm not looking. In the way he stands too close when adjusting my reins, his breath warm against my skin.

This is dangerous territory for both of us. Whit stands to lose more than just his job. If Everett ever found out, he wouldn't be satisfied with simply firing him—he'd make sure Whit never worked again. His influence stretches far beyond Briarwood Hall, and I have no doubt he would crush Whit without a second thought.

Which is why I have to stop this. I have to stop feeling this way. I cannot let our relationship progress beyond friendship. But every time Whit looks at me, his charm so disarming, I wonder if it's already too late.

August 6, 1970

Everett arrived home early today for the senate break. I wasn't aware he was back until I caught sight of him on the fence line, watching me as I cleared a small series of jumps. Watching me and Whit.

When I landed my final jump perfectly, Whit cheered and clapped, his excitement genuine and unguarded. He hadn't seen Everett either. When Whit finally noticed him, his entire posture changed. The easy smile vanished, replaced by rigid formality.

"Mr. Meyer! Welcome home!" He strode toward Everett, hand extended in greeting. "Your wife is an excellent student. She has a natural talent for riding. I know you must be proud."

Everett didn't shake his hand. Instead, his gaze flicked from me to Whit and back again, as if working through a calculation. A slow, deliberate assessment. The displeasure in his eyes was unmistakable. "She has a lot of work to do if she's to be ready for fox hunting this fall," he said cooly.

The warmth I had felt just moments ago drained away, replaced by something cold and foreboding. When I returned to the house, Everett was waiting for me in our bedroom. Without a word, he ripped off my clothes, the way he had on our honeymoon. He shoved me to the floor, his grip bruising, his body crushing. I closed my eyes, retreating into myself, numbing the pain.

Afterward, as I was cleaning myself up in the bathroom, I noticed a trail of bite marks on my neck. Everett had always been careful not to leave visible marks. But this time he wanted them seen. He had staked his claim on me. For Whit's benefit.

August 7, 1970

Whit was immediately suspicious when I arrived at the barn this morning wearing a turtleneck, despite the warm weather. He questioned me about it, and I forced a laugh, teasing that Everett had given me a hickey. But Whit saw right through the lie. He pulled down my collar just enough to expose the bruises and muttered that they weren't hickeys, asking if my husband routinely bit me. I laugh again, but neither of us thought it was funny.

Whit had planned for us to take a trail ride, saying he had something important to talk to me about, but before we could mount up, Everett emerged from the house. Without acknowledging me, he saddled his own horse and ordered Whit to raise the jumps to their highest setting. Then, with practiced ease, he rode the course flawlessly, as if to remind both of us exactly who he was. When he dismounted, he handed the reins to Whit with a cold, cutting remark—telling me that's what he was paying Whit to teach me. He didn't need to say anything else. The message was clear.

After Everett returned to the house, Whit led his horse into the barn, waiting for it to cool down before finally turning to me. His voice was low when he whispered what I already knew was coming. He told me he could see it in my eyes—that I wasn't happy, that I felt the same way he did. Then he said the words that made my breath catch. Let's run away together. He was willing to give it all up, to risk everything, for me. But I couldn't let him.

I shut him down with an icy glare, telling him the truth in the only way that mattered. Did he really understand what he was asking? Was he prepared to give up his life? Because Everett is a powerful man, one who keeps dangerous company, and I know without a doubt that if Whit and I run, Everett will never stop hunting us. Whatever feelings we have for each other, we have to forget them. It's the only way.

I turned my back on him and walked away, feeling the weight of what I was leaving behind. It was the hardest thing I've ever done. And yet, I know I will have to do it again tomorrow. And the next day. And every day after that.

August 18, 1970

I avoided Whit as much as possible while Everett was home on break. Not just because I was fighting my feelings for him, but because I didn't want him to see the traces of Everett's anger on my face. My husband blames me for not getting pregnant again. As if I have any control over my body. He smacks me around, leaving red welts on my cheeks. The other night, while he was having his way with me, he tried to strangle me. I have bruises in the shape of his fingerprints to prove it.

He's like a volcano, gurgling and churning beneath the surface. I'm terrified of what will happen when he erupts.

Anyway, he's gone now. Away for at least two weeks. And there's good news—Melanie took her very first steps. Everett didn't see them, of course. He was in his study, barking orders into the phone.

Twenty-Seven

2008

I skip breakfast on Monday morning and carry my easel down to the hollow, the damp earth soft beneath my feet. I stare at the blank canvas for hours, the morning light shifting, shadows lengthening. My newfound inspiration—snuffed out beneath the significance of discovery. After reading Mama's diary well into the night, I hardly slept a wink, my mind churning with revelations I hadn't been ready to face. I need solitude now—to sift through her words, to make sense of the woman she was before she became the ghost of my childhood.

I don't blame Mama for loving the horse trainer. She had been drowning in loneliness, starved for kindness, a gentle touch. She fought her desire for him, remaining true to her marriage vows, despite the way my father abused her.

If only I could unsee the truth of the man who was my father.

The need to create, to express, feels hollow in the wake of what I've learned. Even so, I force myself to pick up the brush, to paint, to find solace in my strokes. I focus on a nearby black locust tree, its clusters of white blooms just beginning to unfurl, delicate and unaware of the storms that might come.

But when I step back to take in my work, a chill spreads through me, slow and deliberate, as if the air itself has turned to ice.

The tree is there, but standing among the blooms is a strikingly handsome man with dark, menacing eyes—Everett. Hearing the crunch of tires on gravel in the driveway, I gather my supplies and head up to the house. My steps falter at the sight of my son standing beside his black 4Runner, his pale eyes staring at the house with confusion. He rakes a hand through his dark curls, a habit so familiar it sends a jolt through me. The older he gets, the more he looks like his father.

"Nate! What're you doing here? How did you find me?"

He turns slowly toward me, his expression unreadable. "I've been trying to reach you. But my calls wouldn't go through. I was worried something had happened to you." He yanks a crumpled envelope from his back pocket. "Then I found this in a stack of mail at home."

I recognize the thick cream paper with the attorney's name printed in the return address corner.

Nate gestures toward the house. "So this is it? Your childhood home. Your birthright. Your inheritance."

I keep walking, setting my art supplies down on the edge of the porch. "Yes, son. This is where I grew up."

A flush creeps up his neck, spreading to his face, his features hardening. "Right. With your *family*. The same family I've asked you about my entire life, and you told me they didn't exist. No mother, father, brother, or sister. And I'm so gullible, I believed you." His tone sharpens, cutting me like a blade.

My shoulders sag. "If you'll calm down, I can explain."

Nate lets out a bitter laugh. "Oh, now you want to explain? As if I would believe anything you have to say. You're a liar, mother."

Before I can respond, Blossom appears. Her voice is calm but carries a warning. "Anger's a fire, sweetheart. It'll burn through everything you love if you let it."

Nate turns on her, eyes flashing. "Love? There's no love lost between her and me," he says, aiming his thumb over his shoulder at me.

A sharp pain pierces my chest. "Everything I've done, I've done out of love."

Nate ignores me, suddenly more interested in Blossom. "Who are you anyway? Are you my grandmother?" His gaze shifts back to me. "Is that why you refused to tell me about your family? Because you're ashamed of your biracial parents?"

I shake my head. "No, son. Blossom is my friend. She's been helping me fix up the house." I reach for his hand, but he jerks it away. "I haven't seen my mother since before you were born. She passed away recently. She left no will, so I inherited the house."

Nate grunts, suspicion darkening his expression. "What about my grandfather?"

I bite down on my quivering lip as the reality of everything I've learned about my father crashes down on me. "I never met him. I told you—he died—"

Nate's hand shoots out, stopping me cold. "Don't. I already know about the car accident when you were a baby." He steps closer, his nostrils flaring. "What I don't understand is why you won't tell me who *my* father is. You, of all people— you, who knows exactly how it feels to grow up without a father—how could you do that to me?" His voice drops to a low, dangerous edge. "I'm gonna ask you one more time, Mother. Who is my father?"

From the corner of my eye, I see Sam's truck approach. This is no time to introduce my son to my . . . my *what*? My *boyfriend?* I could drag Nate inside, insist on talking to him in private, but he's clearly in no state to be reasoned with.

Nate waves his hand in front of my face. "Mother! Are you in there? Do you even know who my father is?"

I have been dreading this moment since Nate was born. Sam or no Sam, if I don't tell him the truth *now*, I will lose my son forever.

I inhale a shaky breath, meeting Nate's gaze. "Of course, I know. I kept your father's identity from you . . . to protect my sister's marriage."

Confusion flashes across Nate's face, quickly followed by disbelief. "Are you saying you slept with your sister's husband? You truly are despicable."

My pulse races. "No! Nate! You don't understand. They weren't married at the time . . . He was my boyfriend first."

Nate shakes his head, as though not believing what he's hearing. "And what? Your sister stole him from you?"

"Something like that," I mutter.

"But that makes no sense. If your sister betrayed you, why did you feel the need to protect *her* marriage?"

I bite down on my quivering lip, searching for a response that makes sense. But there is none. After what my sister did to me, I owe Mellie nothing.

Nate rolls his eyes. "Whatever. I don't care about your sister. I want to know about her husband." His voice drops, quiet but razor sharp. "Tell me who he is, Mother? Who is my father?"

My throat tightens around the name. I swallow hard, forcing it out. "Gunner Stone."

Nate's eyes widen. "The famous music producer?"

I lower my head, nodding once, unable to meet his eyes.

A bitter laugh escapes him. "I don't believe you. Do you have any idea what Gunner Stone could've done for my music career? How could you keep this from me?" He throws up his hands. "Not only did you hide my father's identity—you stole my dream."

"I did what I thought best," I whisper.

"For you maybe," Nate snaps, yanking his car door open.

"Not just me. For everyone involved." I reach for him, desperate for him to understand, but he slams the door, nearly crushing my fingers. My heart shatters as he speeds off down the driveway, gravel spitting in his wake.

I barely notice Blossom slipping away, quietly disappearing into the house.

Summoning what little courage I have left, I turn to face Sam.

Disappointment is etched across his face, his lips pressed into a thin line, his blue-gray eyes as stormy as the ocean. "How could you keep your son's father from him?"

Anger flares hot in my chest. How dare he judge me when he knows so little? "There's so much you don't understand, Sam."

He shakes his head. "Your excuse about protecting your sister's marriage doesn't work for me anymore than it did for Nate. What's the real reason you kept your son from his father? Are you afraid of losing him? Afraid that if he knew the truth, he'd abandon you and go to Gunner instead?"

Fear of losing my son. The same thing Blossom accused me of. Everyone sees the truth but me. "This is none of your business, Sam."

"You're right," he says, his voice quiet but firm. "It isn't. But my heart breaks for that boy anyway. I would've given anything to be a father. And here you are, keeping a father and son from knowing each other for selfish reasons." His eyes darken with something like regret. "You're not the person I thought you were."

Sam turns on his heels and walks away, his work boots

crunching over the gravel. As I watch him disappear down the driveway, grief crashes over me like a riptide. My legs buckle, and I collapse, sobs wracking my body. Blossom's arms wrap around me, steady and sure, but I barely feel them as she helps me to my feet and leads me to the porch.

Twenty-Eight

"You were right, Blossom." My voice shakes as the truth descended upon me like a crushing weight. "I kept Nate from his father because I was afraid of losing him. Gunner took Mellie from me—I couldn't afford to lose Nate too." I bury my face in my hands, shame burning in my chest. "I'm a horrible, selfish person. I don't blame God if he strikes me dead."

Blossom's voice is soft but firm. "You're human, Goldie Girl. And God loves you no matter what. You weren't trying to hurt Nate. You were trying to protect what mattered most." She takes my face in her hands. "You suffered a terrible betrayal, not just from the boy you loved but also from your own sister. Your trusted sibling. It's only natural to fear losing your beloved son too."

She eases me into the rocker. "Sit right here and don't you move. I'm going to fix you some of my special nerve-calming tea."

She's barely disappeared inside when I'm back on my feet, pacing the porch in frantic circles, gnawing my nails as I stab at Nate's number again and again. Straight to voicemail. My pulse roars in my ears, every worst-case scenario rushing in—

he's driving too fast, upset with me, loses control, slams into a tree.

I sink into the chair, defeated, and toss the phone onto the table with a groan of frustration. He has to be okay. He just *has* to be.

Blossom returns, placing a tray on the table between us. "Feeling any better?"

"No! Nate isn't answering his phone." I press my palms hard against my temples, willing my thoughts to calm. "I have to do something. I need to warn my sister, but she won't accept my calls."

I bolt upright in my chair. "Maybe she will in the event of an emergency." I tap Mellie's office number into my phone. I recognize the receptionist. By now, I know all their voices. In my mind, this one has mousy brown hair pulled back into a bun, her face perpetually pinched—like she's always struggling to poop.

"This is Lydia Meyer again, calling for my sister." I grip the phone tighter. "Please tell Melanie it's a matter of life and death. And this time it is."

"Whose life or death?" The receptionist's voice sharpens, edged with suspicion.

"Her nephew. Her husband's son." I say, my eyes on Blossom. She gives me a small nod of approval.

A laugh of disbelief bursts over the line. "Seriously, lady? You expect me to believe that?"

"I don't care what you believe. Just give her the message. Tell her to call me back as soon as possible." I recite my cell number before hanging up.

The seconds tick off on my watch. Ten minutes crawl by before my phone finally rings—unknown number. "Mellie? Is this you?"

"What's going on, Liddy? I got an urgent message to call you, that your son's life is in jeopardy. Is this true?"

I spring to my feet and start pacing again. "He's Gunner's son—conceived when he and I were together, before you ran off with him. His life isn't exactly in danger . . . although it may be. I'm not sure. He was really upset when he left here. Anyway, I needed to warn you. Nate just found out Gunner is his father. I have a feeling he's on his way to New York to see him."

A pause. Then Mellie's voice, even but clipped. "What do you mean, he just found out?"

I stop pacing. Something in her tone feels off. Not surprised. Not even rattled. Just cautious.

"For the sake of your marriage, I kept Gunner's identity a secret from my son."

Mellie exhales, the sound slow and deliberate. "Well, that was probably for the best."

I frown. "That's all you have to say?"

Silence fills the line, followed by a tapping of her fingernail against a desk. When she speaks again, she's all business. "Gunner's in Los Angeles this week. He splits his time between the office there and the one here. I'll have his assistant keep an eye out in case your son calls."

I wait, expecting more. An explanation. A question. Anything.

But the line goes dead.

I stare at the phone, dazed and confused. "That was . . . weird."

"Are you surprised? You two haven't spoken in over twenty years."

"She seemed unfazed when I told her Gunner and I had a son—almost as if she already knew."

"Maybe she was just being cautious," Blossom suggests.

"Maybe." I press the back of my hand to my forehead. "I don't feel well. I need to lie down," I say, stumbling toward the door, my new reality pressing down on me like an anchor.

I take to my bed, much like I did all those years ago when Mellie and Gunner disappeared together. I lie perfectly still and pray for peace, but my mind, caught in a relentless loop of memories, refuses to be tamed.

It's not Nate who dominates my thoughts though. It's Mellie.

She called me *Liddy* on the phone—as though we'd last seen each other just yesterday, not twenty-two years ago. What happened to us? We'd once been inseparable. And then she pushed me away.

After she discovered the cemetery, something changed. She withdrew, pulling further and further from me. And then, on her thirteenth birthday, something happened. Something that seemed to shake her to her core.

I was there that night—I witnessed her argument with Mama. Although I never understood what it was about.

The past collides with the present, flashes of memory rushing at me so fast and furious that I can't separate them anymore. I squeeze my eyes shut, desperate for sleep. But whenever I drift off, the nightmares come.

Twenty-Nine

1982

I was caught outside in a storm. Someone was chasing me through the woods. I ran as fast as I could, branches clawing my face, rain soaking my skin. But no matter which way I turned, I couldn't find my way out.

I woke with a gasp, panting and drenched in sweat, my heart hammering against my chest. Just a dream.

The house was silent—no thunder, no pounding rain. Through the open window, the full moon hung in a star-drenched sky, casting an eerie glow across the room.

I threw back the covers and padded across the hallway to Mellie's room. Her bed was empty. I pressed my hand to the sheets. Cold. She hadn't slept here in hours.

Where could she have gone?

We turned in around nine o'clock, after her birthday dinner, such as it was—a dry slice of cornbread, a bowl of vegetable soup, and a store-bought cake, lopsided with her name misspelled in smeared icing.

Moving to the window, I rubbed the sleep from my eyes. Light flickered from the clearing in the field. I squinted.

Was that Mama? And Mellie?

Why were they having a bonfire in August? In the middle of the night.

Something was wrong.

Spinning away from the window, I flew down the stairs and out of the house, my yellow nightgown billowing behind me. Mellie's sobs grew louder as I ran toward the clearing, crouching low through the neat rows of summer crops.

They were arguing—screaming things I didn't understand.

"This is crazy, Mama. You're crazy. A crazy bitch."

The panic in Mellie's voice sent me to my knees. I'd never heard my sister curse before.

I crawled the rest of the way, my breath coming in panicked gasps. When I reached the clearing, I clamped a hand over my mouth to stifle a cry.

Mellie was seated in a kitchen chair, her arms and legs bound with rope. Mama loomed over her, brandishing a glowing iron poker like a sword, her hazel eyes wild and blazing with something I didn't recognize, something that terrified me.

"This isn't a punishment, Melanie. This is your birthright —your induction into the society."

"I don't wanna be in your barbaric society. You have the evidence—use it against them. Save me from this madness! I'm your daughter. Choose me over them!"

I watched in horror as Mama pressed the poker to my sister's wrist. Mellie threw back her head and let out a blood-curdling scream that made my flesh crawl.

Panic clawed at my chest. I was too small. Too weak. Powerless.

Heart pounding, I scrambled to my feet and raced through the crops, bare soles sinking into damp soil, nightgown catching on stalks of corn—ripping as I tore it free.

When I reached the house, I slammed the door shut

behind me and collapsed against it, my lungs burning and face wet with tears.

Then I froze.

I had left Mellie. But how was an eleven-year-old supposed to save her sister from their evil mother? We had no phone to call for help. I was too young to drive the truck. And our nearest neighbor was miles away. There was nothing I could do.

A horrific thought struck me—cold and sharp as a blade. What if Mama came for me next?

I tore up the stairs, taking them two at a time, and threw myself onto the bed. Yanking the covers over my head, I folded myself into a ball, squeezing my eyes shut.

Maybe if I hid deep enough, the nightmare would disappear. Maybe Mama couldn't find me.

A loud bang echoed through the house—the front door slamming shut. Heavy footsteps pounded up the stairs. My heart raced as I held my breath and waited.

After a long minute, I pushed back the covers and tiptoed to the door, cracking it just enough to see into the hallway. Mama's door was closed. But Mellie's stood ajar, and I could hear her soft sobs.

I tapped lightly. "Mellie? Are you okay?"

A beat of silence. Then—"Go away," she shouted.

I slipped inside anyway and crept toward the bed. Mellie was curled up, her body trembling as she cradled her left hand. I leaned over her shoulder, and I gasped when I saw the angry red mark on her wrist.

"Do you want me to get some ice for that?"

Mellie jerked upright. "No, Liddy! I told you to go away!"

I stumbled back from the bed. "I'm so sorry, Mellie. I should've tried to save you, but I was too scared. I'm just a fraidy cat—like Mama says."

She glared at me through swollen eyes. "For once, this isn't about you."

I pressed my fist to my mouth, blinking back tears. "I don't understand. Why did she do that to you? Why did she hurt you?"

Mellie turned her face away. "Trust me, you don't want to know. Now, get out." Her arm shot out, finger pointed at the door.

"But—"

"Now, Liddy!"

"Okay."

Tears streamed down my cheeks as I backed out of the room.

I never minded that my life differed from other children's. I loved Marsh Hollow—its peacefulness, its sense of home. But as I crawled back into bed, a sick feeling spread through my gut. Even though I was only eleven, I understood one thing for sure. Our lives had changed tonight. And not for the better.

Thirty

2008

I jerk awake, heart pounding. Through the window, dark clouds hang low, streaks of lightning flashed in the distance.

What time is it? What day is it? Tuesday? No, it must be Wednesday at least.

Throwing my legs over the side of the bed, I pull on the clothes I was wearing when Nate was here—a pair of black yoga pants and a lightweight sweatshirt.

When I step into the upstairs hall, I hear Blossom banging around in the kitchen, making yet another meal I won't touch.

I slip out the front door, walking in a daze toward the field, the nightmare still vivid in my mind.

Mellie had screamed: *You have the evidence—use it against them!*

What evidence? Did Mama know something damning about the Dominion Society?

Memories churn, rushing back faster than I can process.

Mellie kept her wrist wrapped in gauze for weeks. When the bandages finally came off, long-sleeved shirts took their place. But I still caught fleeting glimpses of the wound as it healed—red blisters hardening into blackened skin. And then the letters emerged—*D* and *V*.

Over time, the mark faded, but it never disappeared. Then, when Mellie began making jewelry, she wove a thick, braided leather strap and secured it around her wrist—a permanent bracelet that shielded the scar from sight.

I stop in the clearing where the bonfire once burned, my thoughts racing. Pieces of the puzzle are falling into place— fragments from Mama's journals and sparks of memory I've kept buried. As the firstborn, Mellie would have been initiated into the Dominion Society. But what exactly did she need saving from? Was Mama arranging a marriage for her—with another first-born from the Society?

I'm so lost in thought I don't hear Blossom calling for me. It's not until the earth beneath my feet vibrates that I look up and see it—a funnel cloud, slicing across the field, barreling straight toward me.

Fear locks me into place, steals my voice. Then—bam—a force slams into me from behind, knocking me flat. The impact drives the air from my lungs. Gasping, I struggle against the weight pinning me down.

Blossom's voice is near my ear. "Hold still, Goldie Girl. Don't move."

I wait, heart pounding. I'm certain this is it. Any second now, the tornado will scoop us up, toss us like rag dolls, and hurl us into the bay.

A crushing pressure builds in my ears, ringing so loud I can barely think. My head throbs like it might split in two.

Then, as suddenly as it came, the tornado is gone.

An eerie silence falls over us. After a long minute, Blossom rolls off of me. "Good Lord have mercy. I thought for a moment I was a goner."

I look over at her. "I thought you were already dead."

Blossom lets out a humph. "I may be on heaven's payroll, but tornado duty wasn't in the job description."

We lie there together, side by side, staring up at the clearing sky, collecting ourselves. Finally, she gets up and helps me to my feet, brushing the dirt off my clothes. Blossom's gaze shifts, locking on something behind me. "Would you look at that?"

I whirl around, a cold wave of dread crashing over me. The front section of the forest has been stripped away. Trees lie snapped like matchsticks, the ground littered with broken branches and upturned earth.

And there, in all its naked glory, is the Malone family cemetery.

"Do you think this is a sign?" I ask, stunned.

"Maybe." Blossom nods slowly. "I've been praying my old heart out for guidance. That stand of pine trees is gone, and your family cemetery is exposed for all the world to see. I believe someone's trying to tell you not to hide your family history. To be proud of it."

Before I can respond, the crunch of gravel announces the arrival of a blue pickup truck.

My stomach drops. *Sam.* He's the last person I ever expected to see on my property again.

Tearing around the bend, he skids to a halt, jumps out, and jogs toward us. "Are y'all okay?" He scans us from head to toe. "I saw the whole thing from my front yard. Couldn't believe my eyes. Scared me half to death."

The enormity of what just happened finally crashes over me. The nightmare. The tornado. My close brush with death.

My legs buckle as I burst into tears. Arms engulf me, strong and steady. I bury my face against a solid chest, sobs shaking my shoulders. But it's not Blossom holding me. It's Sam.

I shrink back, eyes darting around. "Where did Blossom go?"

Sam glances over his shoulder, then back at me, his brow furrowed. "I don't know. She just disappeared. What's her story anyway? Something is . . . different about her."

A soft smile curves my lips. "Something is . . . wonderfully different about her."

He drops his arms from around me, and silence drifts between us as we stare at the destruction. "I know a good land-clearing service if you need one," he offers.

I nod but don't commit. "I'll keep that in mind." A land-clearing service sounds expensive, and most of the damage is contained to the woods.

Sam turns back toward her, his expression hesitant. "I've been hoping for an opportunity to talk to you. I owe you an apology. I know nothing about your relationship with your son, and I was wrong to judge you."

I swallow hard. "But you were right. I used my sister's marriage as an excuse. I'd already lost Melanie to Gunner, and all these years, I've been terrified of losing my son to him too. That fear has cost me our relationship. I don't know where Nate is . . . or if I'll ever see him again."

Sam steps closer, then pulls me into his arms. This time I don't struggle.

"You'll see him again," Sam murmurs. "I can help you look for him, if you'd like."

I lean into him for a moment—just long enough to remember. His scent. His warmth. The way his strong arms once made me feel safe. But I'll never forget how easily he turned against me when I needed him the most. And I'm not sure I can forgive him.

"I can't do this," I say, pushing him away.

A shadow of hurt crosses his face. "You're still sore at me."

"At the risk of throwing your words back in your face,

you're not the person I thought you were." I meet his gaze, my voice steady. "I need a man who always has my back, no matter the circumstances. Who understands that I'm human. Who stands by me when I make mistakes—instead of judging me. Instead of walking away."

Sam's voice is quiet but firm. "I'm human too, Lydia. I admit I was wrong to judge you." He pauses, running a hand through his sandy hair. "I'm overly sensitive when it comes to family. My wife and unborn child were taken from me in the cruelest way." His gaze meets mine, raw with emotion. "So when I saw you keeping something so big from your son, I reacted. Poorly. But it wasn't just about you—it was about me, about what I've lost."

I soften, but only slightly. I know Sam's pain is real, that it has shaped him in ways I can't fully understand. "I'm sorry for what you've been through, Sam. I can't imagine that kind of loss." I swallow, my voice quieter now. "But it doesn't change the fact that you turned your back on me when I needed you most."

His jaw stiffens, but he nods. "I know."

I cross my arms, protecting myself from the pull of his grief—and from the part of me that wants to reach for him. "I get why you reacted the way you did. But that doesn't make it hurt any less." I pause. "Thanks for stopping by."

Turning away, I walk toward the house, a stabbing pain in my chest—like a blade piercing straight through my heart.

I made the dreaded mistake of trusting another man, and he failed me, just as Gunner had failed me twenty-two years ago. I should be grateful it happened early, before I got in too deep, before there was no way out with my dignity intact. But that knowledge does little to dull the sting of betrayal.

I've barely reached the porch when a sheriff's car pulls slowly up beside me. A uniformed young man, his baby face belying his manly build, unfolds himself from the driver's seat. He removes his campaign hat, holding it to his chest. "Afternoon, ma'am. I'm Deputy Sheriff Cal Bennett. Just making the rounds. We saw the twister come through here, and I wanted to check in, make sure you're all right."

"I'm fine, but I appreciate your concern, Deputy Bennett."

"Please, call me Cal. You must be Aurelia's daughter. I helped locate you after your mama's passing."

Confusion pinches my face at first, then I remember. "Oh, right. Marge mentioned a local deputy had taken a special interest in the case."

"That's me." He tilts his head, studying me. "Are you the jewelry designer?"

"No, I'm the younger sister. Lydia Meyer." My legs feel weak again, but I can't let him get away. "Arthur Pendleton promised to send someone from your office to talk to me about my mother's death. I take it that's not you?"

He shakes his head. "Not me. But I can spare a few minutes, if you have questions. What's on your mind?"

"I'd like to see the autopsy report. My mom was relatively young to have died of natural causes."

Cal gives me a look that says he agrees with me, but his words surprise me. "I'm sorry. I can't show it to you."

My brow shoots up. "Why not? Is it top secret or something?"

"Something." He appears conflicted, as though unsure of how much to say. "The medical examiner never performed an autopsy."

"What?" I say, my voice rising. "Marge told me the sheriff sealed off the house. Why would he investigate and not do an autopsy?"

Cal glances around, suddenly seeming nervous.

"Cal? Is everything okay?"

"Let's take a walk. I'd like to check out your storm damage."

"Okay." I would follow him to Mars if it meant finding answers about my mother's death.

The periwinkle sky stretches out ahead of us as we stroll across the field. It's hard to believe a tornado came through here less than an hour ago.

I wait until we're out of earshot of the house. "I don't understand. The intruders trashed her house. Painted graffiti on her walls. They may have murdered her. Why didn't the sheriff order an autopsy?"

"The same reason he didn't investigate."

I wait for him to say more, but he remains quiet, as though uncertain whether to trust me. I try another tactic. "What reason is that? Based on the nature of the graffiti, I think it's safe to assume that someone associated with the Dominion Society broke in. Maybe one of their Watchmen?"

Cal stops walking. "You know about Do-Do-Dominion? About th-th-the Watchmen," he says, stuttering a little.

I nod curtly. "I'm just learning about them."

He hesitates, as though he's going to say something, then heads off again. I quicken my pace to fall into step beside him.

"My father was sheriff in this county," Cal says. "And his father before him. I aim to follow in their footsteps one day."

I'm not sure where he's going with this, but I let him talk.

"The Dominion Five, the Elders, are powerful men. They're not to be messed with. They control the society." His chuckle is tinged with sarcasm. "Really and truly, they control the whole Commonwealth of Virginia."

"Do they control your department?" I ask on a hunch.

"Law enforcement officers have taken bribes from them—

to cover up crimes committed by the society. Some are as simple as speeding tickets. Others are more serious."

"And you? Do you take bribes?"

He grimaces, as though experiencing pain. "I've looked the other way a time or two. But only because they left me no other choice. Taking down the Elders has been a lifelong dream of mine. If only I had the goods . . ."

I sense he's holding something back, but I don't press him.

Cal kicks at the dirt. "The Watchmen always leave their seal at the crime scene. It's a warning to authorities not to get involved. That's why no one investigated Aurelia's death."

I remember Marge's reaction when I mentioned the graffiti. *Our crew was supposed to remove that.* "I don't understand. Why would they kill a sixty-four-year-old midwife?"

Cal inhales an unsteady breath, as though revealing this truth might change everything. "Aurelia may have known something. Or maybe she was hiding evidence. After all, she was married to Everett Meyer—the most powerful elder of them all."

Last night's dream rushes back to me. *You have the evidence—use it against them!* "But Everett's been dead for decades. Why kill her now?"

"I've heard rumors she was losing her mind." He taps his temple. "Saying the wrong things to the wrong people."

"That makes sense. If the Watchmen didn't find what they were looking for, they may come back. Which means no one is safe, living here." My gaze shifts toward the barn. "I've been avoiding Mama's office. As kids, we were forbidden to go in there. Do you know if anyone checked it?"

He follows my gaze. "I poked around in there. All that's left is a black metal desk. Someone—either Aurelia or the people who broke in—cleared everything out."

We reach the edge of the woods and stand in silence, surveying the damage.

"Thank you for being honest with me, Cal."

He turns to me, his campaign hat tucked under one arm, his face somber. "You deserved the truth. Your mama deserved better."

I nod. "If I find anything, I'll let you know."

"Be careful, Lydia," he says, his voice low. "The Elders don't play fair. And you're Everett's daughter. I don't know if that protects you or makes you a target."

Slipping his hat on his head, he starts back across the field. I watch him go, a strange heaviness settling in my chest.

The storm might've passed—but something tells me the real danger is just beginning.

Thirty-One

Instead of returning to the house, I go down to the dock to clear my head. I'm sitting with my legs dangling over the side, watching minnows dart beneath the water's surface, when Blossom eases, moaning and groaning, down beside me.

"I tried coaxing. I tried tea. All it took was a twister to get you outta bed," she says, nudging me with her elbow.

I force a smile. I appreciate her attempt at humor, but I'm not in the mood to laugh. "Thank you for saving my life. That twister would've carried me off to Timbuktu if you hadn't been there."

Blossom smooths my hair back from my face. "I'm just glad you're feeling better. Wallowing in self-pity won't help nobody. Least of all yourself."

"I wish I'd hear from Nate. I need to know he's safe."

"I have a hunch Nate will eventually come around. Mellie too. And when they do, you need to present your best self to them."

I roll my eyes. "Here comes the lecture on the meaning of happiness. Don't you have some other lost soul's life to save?"

Blossom cackles. "I'm not done with you yet." She situates

s herself, crossing her ankles and leaning back on her hands. "Know what I think?"

I cut my eyes at her. "I have no clue."

She pauses, choosing her words. "The way I see it, you have all the makings of a fresh start."

"Really? This doesn't feel like a fresh start to me. What exactly are these *makings*?" I ask, my voice heavy with doubt.

Blossom sweeps an arm toward the farmhouse. "This place. Whether or not you realize it, Marsh Hollow is in your heart. Your minor renovations have made a major impact. The house is beginning to feel like you—*your* home. And your talent. It's a gift from God, Goldie Girl. While you were sequestered in your room, indulging in your pity party, I took the liberty of looking around your studio. You have a unique style that goes beyond landscapes. You could design stationery, book covers, even home décor. The possibilities are endless if you'd open yourself to them."

Her suggestions awaken glimmers of hope inside me. I've never considered exploring other avenues for my art. "I'll think about it." I lean back against a piling, my arms wrapped snuggly around my knees. "As for the house, I'm not sure I can stay at Marsh Hollow after all." I tell her about my dream and conversation with Deputy Bennett. "If there is evidence hidden on this property, the Elders won't be happy until they find it. Which means I'm not safe here."

Blossom levels her gaze on me. "Then we need to find that evidence."

I retreat to my studio after breakfast on Thursday to explore new directions for my art. But nothing stirs me like landscapes—the simple, meditative act of transferring a vision to canvas, capturing a moment only I can see. Still, the thought of designing luxury fabrics for high-end interiors intrigues me.

I'm sketching an all-over pattern for a printed fabric when a banging rattles the front door downstairs. Before I can push back from my desk, the pounding resumes—this time accompanied by a voice as familiar as my own skin, though I haven't heard it in over twenty years.

"Liddy! Open up! I know you're in there!"

I freeze. Even after she ignored all my desperate attempts to reach her, some part of me always knew she'd come.

I drop the pink colored pencil on my worktable and stand clumsily, inhaling a deep breath. *Ready or not, here we go.*

Mellie is as stunning as ever—sophisticated and poised, exactly what one would expect from a successful jewelry designer. Her luscious thick auburn hair is swept into a messy updo, and her elegantly cut black pantsuit paired with a white silk blouse exude effortless refinement.

She gives me a quick once-over, her lips pressed into a thin line. "God, I hate this place. Why'd you have to drag me down here? You got any whiskey?"

"Um . . . Yes, but it's ten o'clock in the morning."

Mellie waves a dismissive hand, nearly losing her balance before catching herself on the arm of a chair. "Drunk's the only way I can tolerate being here."

She brushes past me into the living room, the pungent scent of whiskey trailing her. She's clearly already been drinking—probably drunk. Did she start on the flight from New York? Or worse, did she drive herself from the airport in this condition?

I stick my head out the door, scanning the driveway. No rental car. Glancing back, I watch Mellie circle the room, dragging her fingers along the new furnishings. No suitcase either. Just one oversized black tote slung over her shoulder. She's not planning to stay.

"How did you get here?" I ask, closing the door behind me.

"Taxi." Mellie gestures at the room with a sweeping motion. "What's all this? Are you the lady of the manor now?"

"The house was wrecked when I arrived. And since you disclaimed it, someone had to take responsibility for cleaning it up. A fresh coat of paint really helped. Mama hadn't changed a thing in all these years."

Mellie's mouth twists, mocking and unkind. "*Mama*. You always were Mama's little girl."

The pressure of unshed tears burns behind my eyelids, but I refuse to blink, refuse to let Mellie get to me. I clench my jaw, forcing the words out evenly. "I learned early on how to stay out of trouble."

"And I learned early how to fight back," Mellie snaps, striding toward the kitchen, her four-inch heels cracking against the hardwood like a judge's gavel.

I follow my sister into the kitchen, stopping in the doorway as Mellie yanks open cabinets and slams them shut again. "Check the one to the right of the refrigerator."

Mellie locates the whiskey, unscrews the cap, and drinks straight from the bottle. She smacks her lips. "Ahh."

I bite back the comment on my tongue. My sister is in a foul mood. Criticizing her will only make it worse.

She turns to me, eyes bloodshot and burning. "Gunner never loved you, you know? You were a fool to have his baby. Were you hoping he'd leave me and come running back to you?"

I grip the doorjamb, steadying myself. "If I'd wanted that, I would've found you, told you about the baby. But I didn't want to interfere in your marriage."

She points the bottle at me like it's loaded. "Then why are you trying to ruin my marriage now?"

"I'm not. Nate found a letter from the estate attorney. I had no choice but to tell him the truth."

Mellie takes another swig of bourbon. "I've known about your bastard child all along."

So she did know about Nate.

"Gunner told me he'd slept with you, stolen your virginity down in the hollow. Sounds like lyrics for a cheesy country music song. Thank goodness Gunner never wrote about you." She chugs again and lets out a loud belch. "I worried he might have gotten you pregnant, and I hired a team of private investigators. They've been keeping tabs on you all these years. As a preventative measure. In case you showed up out of the blue. Like now."

I stare at her, dumbfounded. "But you never told Gunner?"

"Nope. For the same reason you never did." She digs her index finger into my chest. "It would've made life messy for everyone."

"So you let me raise him by myself instead. At great cost to me, by the way. My son resents me for keeping his paternity from him."

"Children are a distraction, Liddy. I couldn't let your son interfere with Gunner's road to success." She waves the bottle wildly, bourbon sloshing onto the floor. "You're the perfect example. You've been a waitress all your life. Gunner and I achieved great things without the burden of having a family."

I shake my head in disbelief. The person standing in front of me is not the Mellie I remember. Or is she? Had I put her on a pedestal, refusing to see her flaws because I loved her too much? "Is that why you never had children?"

She lifts the bottle again, guzzling without pause. "Gunner wanted a family. But I made sure we never had kids."

I blink hard. "You mean you tricked him?"

"If you want to call it that. I just kept taking my birth

control pills, and he never confronted me about it. When we had trouble conceiving, he just accepted it wasn't meant to be for us." Mellie barks out a laugh, high pitched and brittle, like glass cracking under pressure.

"Give me that." I snatch the bottle away, but Mellie rips it back, spilling liquor down the front of her blouse.

I breathe in and out as I count to ten. I need to defuse the situation, talk her down off the ledge. I soften my voice. "What happened, Mellie? You always wanted children when we were growing up."

"I refused to pass the genes of a batshit crazy woman and a corrupt mob boss to an innocent child." Mellie runs a hand over my hair. "Poor little golden girl. So many family secrets you never knew about."

She smiles, almost tender—then yanks a strand of my hair so hard I cry out.

"No one ever told you. We all thought you were too weak to handle the truth. Fraidy cat."

Tears sting my eyes, but I don't give into them. "I may not have known about all the secrets before, but I'm learning about them now." With one hand pressed to my throbbing scalp, I open a drawer and plunk Mama's fourth and final journal down on the table. "I've read the first three. I'm almost afraid to find out how this tragic story ends."

Mellie's face goes ashen. "Where'd you get that?"

"From the secret compartment inside Ambrose Malone's statue. Now I know why you were so obsessed with the cemetery."

Mellie sets the whiskey bottle down with a thud and picks up the journal. She opens the cover, running her fingers across the first page. Over her shoulder, I see it—the *DV* seal, embossed in a blob of deep-red wax. The other three journals don't have this mark.

Her hand drifts to the inside of her left wrist, fingers

brushing the skin where the brand used to be. In its place is a smooth, raised scar—pink and slightly puckered, the ghost of something she paid to erase.

"Take it away!" Mellie shrieks, flinging her arm out. The diary collides with the whiskey bottle, sending the bottle crashing to the floor. Shards of glass skid across the ancient floorboards, golden liquor spreading in jagged rivulets.

She collapses into the puddle, curling into herself, arms wrapped around her knees. Her whole body shakes violently, her breath coming in short, sharp gasps.

I kneel beside my sister, gently resting a hand on her arm. "Mellie, take a breath. You're hysterical."

"Get away from me," Mellie says, her voice nearing delirium. "I knew it was a bad idea to come here. I should've stayed in New York. I've spent my whole adult life trying to forget the past, and you made it all come crashing back in one day."

Her eyelids droop, and she mumbles something unintelligible. I tap Mellie's face but get no response.

The back door flies open, and Blossom barges in. "What in the Sam Hill?"

"Help me, Blossom. I think she's passing out. We need to get her to the sofa."

Without hesitation, Blossom scoops Mellie up, tossing her over her shoulder like a rag doll, and carries her into the living room.

I dash upstairs for a blanket and pillow. By the time I return, Mellie is snoring softly, her body limp. I gently slide the pillow beneath her head while Blossom tucks the blanket around her.

I press a hand to my chest, my heart still pounding. "She scared me."

Blossom stares down at Mellie. "Looks to me like this girl's got some emotional problems."

"She had a lot to drink. How much did you hear?"

"Most of it. The kitchen window was open. I couldn't help but eavesdrop."

I roll my eyes. "Right. I didn't open the window. Did you?"

Blossom lifted her hands in a helpless gesture. "I may have earlier. I was baking a cake, and it got awfully stuffy in there."

"While she's napping, I'm going to clean the kitchen and then read Mama's last journal. I'm afraid to find out what earth-shattering revelations await me, but I need to know what I'm dealing with."

Blossom opens the front door. "You go on. Find yourself a comfortable spot outside—maybe on the dock or down in the hollow. Somewhere the truth can breathe." Blossom gives me a pointed look. "I'll clean up the kitchen and keep an eye on Sleeping Beauty here."

AURELIA'S JOURNAL 4

September 8, 1970

I had a long talk with Whit today after my lesson. I made it clear we can never be together. Not for lack of want, but for his safety and mine. He hates seeing me like this, trapped in a life that's crushing me, and he begged me to run away with him. He swore he knew of a safe place where Everett could never find me, where I could finally be free.

But I can't take that chance. I won't. I can't put Whit in harm's way, can't bear the thought of something happening to him because of me. I've learned from all my late-night spying missions exactly what my husband's capable of. I can't let Whit suffer because of me. I would never forgive myself if something happened to him.

Because I do love him. I've fallen in love with him. And loving someone means knowing when to hold on—and when to set them free.

I suggested he leave Briarwood, to find another job somewhere far away. But Whit refused. Even if we can't be together, he wants to stay close—just in case I need him.

Like me, he senses it. Something is coming. A storm on

the horizon, inevitable and unstoppable. We feel it bearing down on us, but we're powerless to do anything but wait.

September 15, 1970

The storm has come and gone, but all that remains is ruin and regret.

Everett had barreled in Friday night, unannounced, his temper blazing. I still don't know what set him off. He accused me of having an affair with Whit, of deliberately trying not to get pregnant, of failing him as a politician's wife. Something inside me snapped. Instead of taking his abuse like I always do, I fought back. I gave him a dose of his own medicine.

He didn't take it well. He is much stronger than me, and he beat my face black and blue. When I finally broke free, I fled into the night, running blindly until I reached the barn. I hid in Magnolia's stall, pressing my bruised cheek against her warm coat, my hands shaking as I clung to her. We've bonded these past few months. She's loyal, reliable. I wanted to believe she would protect me from my husband.

But it wasn't Everett who found me. It was Whit. He pulled me into his arms and held me while I sobbed, whispering over and over, "You're safe now. He's gone. I saw his car drive away."

When the tears finally stopped, he carried me upstairs to his apartment above the garage. He did more than just comfort me. He made love to me.

September 18, 1970

My heart is broken. After days of soul searching, this morning, I told Whit it can never happen again. Friday night was a mistake—a beautiful, needed, inevitable mistake—but a mistake all the same.

He didn't argue. He just looked at me, his jaw tight, his eyes heavy with something deeper than disappointment. Maybe he knew I would say it before I even opened my mouth. Maybe he was waiting, hoping I wouldn't.

But I had to. Everett will kill him if he finds out. And if he doesn't kill him, he'll make sure Whit wishes he were dead. I won't be the reason his life is destroyed.

Worried about my safety, Whit offered to teach me how to shoot. I reminded him that I grew up on a farm. My father, an expert marksman, made sure I could handle any weapon. Handguns, shotguns, rifles—I learned them all.

Everett, a weapons collector, has guns all over the house. Most are locked in his gun safes. Though he keeps a loaded pistol in his bedside table and another in his top desk drawer.

October 20, 1970

After more than a month of silence, Everett arrived out of the blue on Friday afternoon. Why the separation? Because he couldn't stomach the sight of my battered face. And because he was testing me, to see if he could dig up dirt on Whit and me. He's paying his staff to spy on me. They're around every corner, all smiles and folded napkins, but their eyes never stop following me.

I'm in the clear for now. There was only the one night, which no one seems to know about.

Everett apologized, begged, pleaded. Then came the gifts —a lavish display of remorse. A bouquet of white orchids, a diamond bracelet I'd once admired in a magazine, and the promise of an African safari next summer. The safari is more for him, not me. But our peers rave about the luxurious wildlife conservation safaris, and for a moment, I let myself imagine the escape.

But I made him squirm. I told him I would think about it. That he had hurt me deeply, and I wasn't sure I could forgive him. For the first time in my life, I have the upper hand, and I like the taste of power.

But in the end, power is an illusion. For my safety and my child's, I will stay married to him. Because I know what would happen if I ever tried to leave.

October 30, 1970

I'm overjoyed—and utterly shattered. Although I have lost the love of my life, I will carry a piece of him forever.

Everett and I haven't resumed marital relations yet. To make up for what he did to me, he insists on courting me again—lavish dinners, thoughtful gifts, letting me decide when to start trying again for another child. I would've waited months. Maybe longer. If not for my missed period.

Now, I have no choice. If I sleep with him soon and claim the baby came early, I might be able to fool him. Might.

Whit's child will grow up as Everett's. And Everett will never know.

November 13, 1970

Friday the thirteenth. A night I wish I could forget.

I never had the slightest hint of morning sickness with my first pregnancy. But this time, it lingers—morning, noon, and night. Somehow, Everett found out. One of the staff must have ratted me out.

I heard his car in the driveway around six o'clock. After

putting Mellie to bed around seven thirty, I went downstairs for dinner and found him in his study, sipping bourbon by a roaring fire. He gestured to the empty chair across from him.

"I understand you haven't been feeling well. Are you pregnant?"

Panic surged through me. I needed more time. It had only been two weeks since we had sex. But I had no choice. I forced a smile.

"Yes! I think so, although it's too early for a test. I was waiting to tell you until I knew for sure."

The whiskey tumbler shattered against the stone fireplace. In an instant, he was on me—fisting my hair, yanking me from the chair, and slamming his fist into my face. Pain exploded through my cheekbone, snapping my head to the side. Before I could recover, another blow landed—then another. My gut, my ribs, my face again. Over and over.

I tried to scream, but the air was knocked out of my lungs.

"Don't waste your breath," he sneered. "No one can hear you. I gave the staff the night off."

That's when I knew. He planned to kill me.

He shoved me against the wall, his hand crushing my throat. My vision blurred, my ears roared. The world slipped away. I was choking . . . fading . . . dying.

Then, from across the room, a faint voice. "Let go of her. Or I'll shoot you dead."

Everett's face flushed scarlet as he turned to Whit, his expression twisting with rage. "You wouldn't dare. You don't have the guts."

Whit didn't blink. "I do when it comes to bastards who abuse women."

He pulled the trigger, and Everett staggered backward, clutching his chest. For a moment, his eyes reflected with disbelief—as if his own downfall had never crossed his mind. Then, with a heavy thud, he collapsed to the floor.

I screamed, dropping beside him, checking his pulse. Nothing. His body was still, the life already drained from him. "You killed him!"

Whit hung his head, his gun pointed at the floor. "If I hadn't come along, he would have killed you. Call the police."

I shot to my feet. "Absolutely not! I can't let you go to jail for murder because of me." Grabbing his arm, I marched him to the foyer. "Hurry! Pack your things. Leave tonight—don't look back."

We argued at the door, but I didn't give in. Whit left reluctantly, and my heart went with him.

As I stood in the doorway, watching him disappear into the night, my mind raced. Calling the police was out of the question. Everett's gun was the same caliber as Whit's, but a ballistic test would prove he was shot with a different weapon. I wasn't worried about myself. I was protecting Whit.

I had only one option. Reginald and Victor. They had covered up Everett's transgressions before. They could make this one disappear too.

Closing the door, I paused at the bottom of the stairs, listening for cries from the nursery. Silence. Returning to Everett's study, I ignored his lifeless body as best I could while I tore the room apart, rifling through drawers, yanking books from shelves, searching for anything that could prove what I already knew.

And then, I found it.

The evidence that could bring the Dominion Society to its knees.

November 14, 1970

I made a deal with the devil, and he came with two faces—Reginald and Victor.

Even with my battered face, they refused to believe I had acted in self-defense. Victor threatened to call the police, convinced the bullet in Everett's chest didn't come from his own gun. *Maybe a certain horse trainer pulled the trigger. I heard you two were having an affair.*

But I was ready. *And I heard you two were involved in Senator Alden's death. In fact, I have evidence to prove it.*

The color drained from their faces. For a moment, I thought Victor might faint.

When they demanded to see the evidence, I laughed at them. *Do you think I'm that stupid? It's hidden somewhere safe. If anything happens to me, a member of the staff will find it and hand it over to the police.*

I placed the evidence in a manila folder and hid it beneath the mattress in the baby's crib. Men rarely looked too closely at a sleeping baby, but if I ended up dead, the nanny would find it.

We struck a deal. I got the short end of the stick, but I'm a young mother, and they are powerful men.

They staged the perfect accident. Everett's car—crashed into the bridge down the road, crumpled but intact. Not enough damage. So they doused the interior with whiskey, slashed a fuel line, and set it ablaze. By the time rescue workers arrived, there wasn't much left to identify.

My punishment is merciless. My inheritance—gone. Everything I'm owed as Everett's widow will be funneled straight into Dominion's coffers. I'm left with nothing. Penniless. And I'm to be exiled, sent back to my parents' farm in disgrace. My future no longer mine to shape.

I am to study under my mother, preparing to take her place as the premier midwife. I will homeschool my children, live off the land, and exist with no social life beyond my family.

The term of my sentence—eighteen years.

If I obey the rules, if I stay quiet, Melanie will have a

future. When she's old enough, she'll be eligible to marry a firstborn, and the Malone family will be back in Dominion's good graces.

May 9, 1971

Six months after I moved home to Marsh Hollow, my parents died, one right after the other, just days apart.

Daddy—a tractor accident.

Mama—a fall from a ladder.

Except Mama had never climbed a ladder in her life.

Beside both bodies, traced into the dirt, was the DV seal.

A warning. A promise. A reminder.

Walk the line. Or I'm next.

Thirty-Three

2008

I close the diary and rest it on my chest, the worn cover rising and falling with each breath. Overhead, the sky is a flawless blue, the sun warm against my face. The scent of jasmine drifts in on the breeze, sweet and persistent, wrapping around me like a memory.

How can a day be so glorious when my heart feels so heavy?

I'm still struggling to wrap my mind around the truth—that Mama slept with Whit, that they'd created a life together, that I am that child. The product of forbidden love. A love that would have cost her everything if it had been discovered. And still, she'd chosen it. She'd chosen him. If only for a moment. She found the kind of love most people spend their whole lives chasing. And then she gave it up. For duty. For survival. For me.

And I'd done the same with Gunner. I loved him, but I let him go. For Mellie. Mama gave up her once-in-a-lifetime love for me. And I gave up mine for my sister. Now I'm the one left holding the pieces.

As the scent of jasmine fills my lungs, I wonder—not for

the first time—how many sacrifices it takes to keep a secret . . . and how many more it takes to finally set it free.

A flicker of hope blooms quietly inside of me. What if my father is still alive?

Despite what Mellie said earlier in her drunken stupor—*Gunner never loved you*—I don't believe her. Gunner did love me, if only for a fleeting moment. Just like Mama and Whit.

I'd been desperate to see my sister. Now I wish I could send her back where she came from. Is she drowning in a full-blown alcohol addiction? Or is she emotionally unstable and self-medicating? Or is she on the verge of insanity like Mama? Either way, I'd hoped for closure. But with Mellie, all I found were more cracks.

I'm drifting off to sleep when I sense someone watching me. I crack an eyelid.

Mellie.

"I could always tell when you were fake sleeping. Your lips do this funny twitching thing." She plops down in the sand beside me. "So this is your hideaway? Isn't that sweet?" She pretends to stick her finger down her throat. "So sweet it makes me want to gag."

I glare at her—this stranger who wears my sister's face but carries none of her softness. She's so bitter. So cynical, like the world chiseled away everything gentle that used to live inside her.

"I was hoping you'd wake up in a better mood."

She grunts. "I won't be in a better mood until I leave this god-awful place. Until I know Gunner is safe. I heard from one of his trusted staff members. Nate showed up at his office in Los Angeles. Now the two of them have disappeared together."

I furrow my brow. "What do you mean, disappeared?"

"Gunner announced he'd be gone for a few days, and they

just left. Didn't say where they were going. I'm hoping they're on the way here. I can't imagine where else they'd be."

I nod. "I hope so too."

"I just took a walk around the property to sober up. This area has really taken off since I was last here—so many new neighbors. Their extravagant homes feel out of place, like they belong in Nantucket or the Hamptons."

"I know what you mean. A real estate developer offered a ridiculous amount of money for Marsh Hollow."

Her eyes widen. "You accepted it, right?"

I shake my head. "I considered it for a minute. But I'd rather sell to a family or retired couple than watch our untamed paradise turned into a gated dreamland for people who'll never appreciate its beauty. Anyway, I'm probably going to move here permanently."

She looks at me as though I've lost my mind. "I would think twice about that, Liddy. This place has bad juju. How much money did he offer you?"

I tell her the amount, and she lets out a low whistle. I can see the wheels already turning. I may not have seen her in twenty-two years, but I know my sister well enough to know she's up to something.

Fanning the pages of Mama's journal, I ask, "When did you find these?"

She shrugs. "I don't remember. I was probably ten or eleven. I found them in Mama's Bible. She'd hollowed out the center, carving a secret space no one would suspect. She never knew what happened to them. Drove her nuts. Crazier than she already was."

I gape at her. "That's just cruel, Mellie. What's even worse, you kept the truth about who I am—who my father really is— all this time."

"I was jealous," Mellie admits in a flat voice. "Mama loved

your father. And you were her favorite child. She loathed my father. And she could barely stand the sight of me."

"That's not true. She expected more of you. Most mothers do of their oldest children. Now that I understand the significance of the firstborn to the Dominion Society . . . it makes even more sense."

Mellie stares into the distance, her hazel eyes fixed on the past. "As the eldest, I was expected to set the standard and sacrifice the most. I was only thirteen when she arranged for me to marry a man twenty years my senior. The wedding was planned for the summer I turned nineteen."

I draw back, eyes wide with surprise. "What? Why didn't you ever tell me?"

Mellie snorts. "I'm surprised you haven't figured it out by now. Then again, you always were a slow learner. Keeping life-altering secrets is one of my many talents."

I ignore her insult, refusing to give her the satisfaction of knowing she got to me. "So you were betrothed just like our father?"

"You mean, *my* father . . . *Betrothed*." She says the word slowly, then shakes her head. "God, I hate that word."

She digs her toes into the sand, burying her feet. "The man was an Elder, as corrupt as my father. I had no control over my future. And I was desperate to get away from Marsh Hollow. And Mama."

"And me," I whisper, barely trusting my voice.

She looks at me, her expression softening, and for a moment, I think she's going to say something kind. But then her face hardens again. "When I saw you and Gunner coming down the stairs together that rainy afternoon, I knew he was my ticket out. I never meant to hurt you, Liddy. You just got in my way."

I wonder if she ever felt even a flicker of guilt. But I'm too afraid to ask.

I blink back the sting behind my eyes. "Do you love Gunner?" I shouldn't care. Not after everything. But I do.

A smile tugs at her lips. "Gunner and I are good together. We complete one another. Our lives work."

I can't bear to think of their lives—the birthday dinners at rooftop restaurants, the concerts, weekend trips to Long Island. Inside jokes, late-night laughs, holidays I spent alone while they played family without me.

"I'm surprised the man you were supposed to marry— your betrothed—let you get away."

"He didn't." Mellie's voice turns brittle. "He came after me. Tracked me down in New York. But I was already married to Gunner by then. There was nothing he could do."

Knowing what I now know about the Elders, sounds like she got off easy. "How much did Arthur Pendleton tell you about Mama's death?"

Mellie appears bored. "Only that she died. I didn't ask questions. I don't want to know."

"Well, you need to know." I give her the rundown of the break-in, the graffiti, and the sheriff's refusal to do an autopsy.

She frowns. I've finally gotten her attention. "Sounds like Dominion."

I run my hand over the leather journal in my lap. "What do you know about the evidence Mama talks about in here?"

Mellie studies my face, pondering her next move. What- ever she sees convinces her I won't let this go. Leaning in, she lowers her voice to a whisper. "You can't repeat this. Not to anyone—especially not Nate or Gunner."

I lean in instinctively.

"My father had a high-tech recording device. The kind spies use. He recorded everything—taped every conversation about his criminal dealings."

I blink slowly, letting this sink in. "How do you know that? Have you actually heard these tapes?"

Mellie nods slowly, her expression unreadable. "Every single word."

"Do you think that's what the intruder was looking for when he broke into the house?"

"Probably. What else would Mama have that anyone would want? Except maybe the records of firstborn births." She sits up straighter. "Mama kept the tapes in a metal box, attached to the underside of her desk with a magnet. Have you been in the barn? Did they ransack her office?"

"I haven't actually gone inside yet," I admit. "But a local deputy who worked the case said her desk is the only thing left. Which means the box might still be there," I say, pushing myself out of the low-slung beach chair.

Mellie shields her eyes from the sun, squinting up at me. "Where are you going?"

"To see if the evidence is still there."

"Easy there, cowgirl." She grabs my wrist, tugging me back down to my chair. "We can't go now. We have to wait . . . until after dinner, until it's dark."

"You think someone's still watching us?"

She scans the horizon, her eyes sharp now, focused. "If they didn't find the evidence when they broke in, you better believe it."

Blossom fries catfish and hushpuppies for our dinner but excuses herself before we sit down to eat. Something about paperwork needing her attention, but I don't buy it. She's giving Mellie and me space. If she senses what we're up to, she doesn't let on.

I reach across the table, offering my hand to Mellie. She takes it hesitantly, her grip uncertain, but she doesn't offer the blessing. When we were young, whenever Mama was away,

Mellie always said the blessing in her place. Her words, spoken from the heart, were beautiful—almost lyrical.

I say a simple blessing instead, and we begin to eat.

"My strong faith has gotten me through some dark times," I say softly. "And I owe that to you, Mellie. All those nights we hid under our beds, terrified by the arguing behind Mama's bedroom door—her harsh words, the voices that didn't sound like her. We prayed together. You quoted Scripture as if you'd written it yourself. You knew the Bible better than anyone I've ever met. Even Mama." I pause. "Do you . . ." My voice trails off.

Mellie doesn't look at me. "Still believe in God? I don't think you ever stop believing. But do I still practice? No."

"Praying every day helps keep me grounded," I say. "It reminds me of what matters."

"Good for you, Liddy." Her voice turns brittle. "God did nothing for me. He certainly never answered my prayers."

"Really?" I ask, trying not to sound too sharp. "Seems to me you got what you wished for. You got your freedom from Mama. You built a life. A successful jewelry company."

Mellie lets out a short, humorless laugh. "*Freedom*, huh? That's one word for it." She pushes her food around on the plate, not eating. "You think success fills the hole Mama left behind?" She glances up, eyes darker than before. "It doesn't."

Neither of us speaks after that. The silence between us says more than either of us is ready to admit.

After cleaning up from dinner, we locate two flashlights in the pantry, check the batteries, and wait until the sky is dark before sneaking off to the barn. It's irrational, maybe, but I half-expect a sniper's red dot to bloom on my chest and drop me in the dirt.

"I've never actually been in Mama's office," I whisper, trailing Mellie through a cluttered maze of ladders, rusty yard tools, and a tractor that hasn't seen the light of day since I was last here.

Mellie stops short, turning toward me in disbelief. "Never?"

I shake my head. "Mama forbid it. Don't you remember? She used to say she'd beat the daylights out of us if she ever caught us in here."

Mellie snorts. "Oh, I remember. She threatened to beat us for everything. But did she ever actually hit you?"

I think for a second, tapping my chin. "No. Not once. Not even when she sent us outside to get switches and we returned with the tiniest twigs we could find."

Mellie grins, a smile that momentarily erases every hard edge. But it's gone in a blink, like it was never there.

She slips a key into the office door's lock. I don't ask where she got it. I'm not sure I want to know.

Inside, Mellie sweeps her flashlight beam over the dust-covered battered desk. "Look under there. Right-hand side, bottom drawer." She shoots me a look that says *well, go on*.

Heart hammering, I drop to my knees and shine the light under the desk. "I don't see anything."

Mellie joins me, crawling beneath the desk and patting around. "It's not here. Either the Watchmen found it, or Mama moved it."

"Great! Now I'll never sleep again. Should I hire armed guards?" I ask as I dust off my pants.

"If I were you, I'd sell the house to the developer, buy a beach bungalow in the Bahamas, and spend the rest of my life sipping rum and working on my tan."

As she locks the door behind us, I murmur, "I don't want to live in the Bahamas." It's too far away from Nate.

Mellie glances toward the house. "Looks like I'm stuck here for tonight. I didn't pack a change of clothes. Can I borrow something to sleep in? I assume my old bedroom is still intact."

I offer a faint smile. "Just as you left it. And I'm sure I can find something clean for you."

"Let's hope Gunner shows up tomorrow." She hugs her arms to her chest. "One night at Marsh Hollow is all I can tolerate. This place gives me the creeps."

For once, I agree with my sister. One night is all *I* can tolerate. Of *her*.

Thirty-Four

On Friday morning, as I tug on my jeans, I allow myself one wicked little fantasy—Blossom making Mellie vanish in the night like a bad dream. But when I come downstairs for breakfast, there she is—alive and well—parked at the kitchen table with her BlackBerry and a steaming cup of coffee, still in yesterday's clothes, the whiskey stain smudged across her white silk blouse.

Disappointment sinks in like day-old grits. Disappointment that she's still here. And disappointment that I feel this way about my own sister.

"What're you working on?" I ask, eyeing the legal pad and pen in front of her.

"I'm making a list of my real estate contacts in New York," she says without looking up. "Marsh Hollow is worth a fortune. If we play our cards right, we could spark a bidding war."

We? My nerves go on high alert. "I already told you, Mellie, I don't want to sell. I'm going to live here. Besides, you disclaimed your inheritance."

She waves a dismissive hand. "I changed my mind."

My temper flares. "You can't do that."

She lifts her chin, her gaze sharpening into a dare. "Says who?"

"Says the law."

"Laws are meant to be broken."

"Not this one." I yank my phone free of my back pocket. "I'll call the estate attorney to confirm." When the call doesn't connect, I head for the door, hoping for better service outside.

"Wait, Liddy! I'll get him on speaker."

She punches in the number and places the BlackBerry on the table. Arthur Pendleton answers on the second ring, his voice groggy with sleep.

"Mr. Pendleton, Melanie Stone," she says in a voice so sweet it could rot teeth. "Sorry for calling so early, but I've decided to reverse my disclaimer. I want my inheritance, after all."

There's a pause, followed by Arthur clearing his throat. "I'm afraid it's too late, Melanie. A disclaimer is irrevocable. You've already signed the papers, and the property has gone to probate."

"But no one told me about the developer's offer," she protests.

"I tried," I cut in. "You wouldn't take my calls. It's too late now–I've decided to stay."

"Please, Arthur!" she whines, a thread of desperation slipping into her voice. "Isn't there *anything* you can do?"

"You could challenge the estate," he says, gently. "But you'd be facing a lengthy legal battle, and you'd likely lose."

"Thanks for nothing," Mellie mutters, pressing a button on her BlackBerry to end the call.

"Seriously, Liddy," she snaps. "You know this isn't fair. We both inherited this property."

"You *disclaimed* your inheritance," I fire back. "You don't get to change your mind because you found out it's worth a lot of money. People aren't pawns, Mellie. You don't get to control them just because it's convenient."

"Control?" she scoffs. "Who have I ever controlled?"

"*Me!*" My voice cracks with fury. "You kept the truth about my father from me for years—decades! And you knew about Nate. You could've told Gunner he had a son, but you kept it from him. On purpose."

She wags her finger at me. "No, Liddy. *You* kept Nate from him."

"For a reason. I was trying to protect *your* marriage." I slam my palm against the table. "But you? You were trying to keep your life neat and tidy. You didn't want Nate interfering with Gunner's success—or your own."

Mellie throws up her hands, voice rising. "I was protecting my marriage too!"

"By lying to your husband? By tricking him into thinking you couldn't have children? You said it yourself, Mellie. You didn't want kids because you were afraid of passing along the genes of your parents."

Our voices thunder through the house, echoing off the walls like gunfire.

Mellie storms to the front door and yanks it open . . . Then freezes. Standing on the porch are Nate and Gunner. Father and son. Identical chestnut curls. Matching crystal-blue eyes. The only thing separating them is twenty-one years.

I gasp, and the blood drains from Mellie's face. "Did you hear all that?" she asks.

Nate's jaw is set, his voice like ice. "Every word."

Shoving them out of the way, Mellie marches out of the house, down the porch steps, and straight down the driveway, past Nate's 4Runner and a black sedan I assume is Gunner's rental.

I look at Gunner. "You should go after her. She doesn't have her bag."

Gunner shakes his head. "I'm not worried about Melanie. She can take care of herself. Besides, I'm sure she has her BlackBerry." His voice is flat, unreadable.

"Aren't you angry about what you heard?"

He exhales, his eyes darkening. "Melanie only thinks about herself. Getting angry won't fix what she did—it'll just eat me alive. Nothing she said surprised me. But I *am* sorry she kept me from my son all these years."

My gaze shifts between them, my son and his father, together at last. "I'm equally to blame."

Gunner offers a small, tired smile. "Maybe. But your intentions were honorable. Melanie was just being vindictive."

Blossom bustles in from the kitchen, wiping her hands on a dish towel. "Lord have mercy, we're having a party, and no one told me." She beams at Nate. "I just pulled a sheet of buttermilk biscuits out of the oven. I bet you could use one."

Nate chuckles nervously. "Actually, I'm not very hungry."

Blossom pats his arm, undeterred. "Growing boy like you? Of course you're hungry. Come on, sugar. Let's you and I get better acquainted." She links her arm through his as if she's known him forever and steers him toward the kitchen.

Gunner watches them go, his expression softening. "He's a fine young man, Lydia. You did a wonderful job with him."

"Thank you." I glance toward the kitchen. "He's my whole world. The one bright spot in a very ordinary life."

He cocks an eyebrow. "Oh. I'm sorry to hear that."

"Don't be. It's not as bad as I make it sound. And it's changing. I'm moving back to Marsh Hollow for good, and I'm finally going to pursue my art career."

Gunner's smile reaches his eyes. "Good for you! Really." He hesitates, then adds, "With all my heart, I wish I'd been part of Nate's life. But after what I did to you, I didn't deserve that chance. Still . . . if it's all right with you, I'd like to get to know him now. Build a relationship if he'll let me."

"He's a grown man, Gunner. You don't need my permission. But for what it's worth, you have my blessing."

He reaches up and gently touches a lock of my hair, letting it fall through his fingers. "You were always the good sister, Lydia. Too good for me. You were the wife I wanted. But Mellie—she was the wife I needed. She's not perfect, but she's been the driving force behind my career. I wouldn't be where I am without her, and I will always be grateful for that."

He sighs, looking down at his hands. "Sure, I wanted children. But I buried that dream a long time ago. I've been consumed by work. On the road constantly. And let's face it—Mellie would've made a terrible mother."

I bite my lip, fighting the smile that threatens to break through.

"I have a lot of making up to do," he says, his voice firm with resolve. "I'll be the father Nate deserves. I promise to be there for him, no matter what."

"I trust you will," I say softly. "He deserves you, Gunner. He's wanted a father all his life. And I deprived him of that."

He squeezes my arm. "We all made mistakes, Lydia. No point dwelling on them now. What matters is what we do next."

"Thank you," I murmur, a lump rising in my throat. "Your kindness means more than you know."

His gaze drifts toward the door. "I should go after Melanie before she gets herself into trouble." He leans in and kisses my cheek. "It was great to see you again. Let's not let another twenty years pass before the next time."

I take him in—his familiar smile, the soft creases at the corners of his eyes, the warmth in his voice. After all these years, I still have feelings for him. Not romantic—those days are gone. He's my sister's husband. But he's also the father of my only child. And despite everything, I want us to be friends.

If Mellie has her way, she'll do everything in her power to keep Gunner from both Nate and me.

"You are always welcome at Marsh Hollow," I say. "Maybe you and Nate can come back for a weekend sometime."

"I'd love that."

I run upstairs to Mellie's room for her bag, then stick my head in the kitchen. "Nate! Come say goodbye to your father."

I follow them outside, waiting on the porch while Nate walks Gunner to his car. They talk for a minute before Gunner pulls him in for a long embrace. My heart overflows with emotion. Sadness because of the time they've lost because of me, but gladness for the time they will now have together because I took a chance on coming here.

As he walks back toward me, Nate swipes at his eyes, but when he reaches me, his smile is broad, a smile I've rarely seen from him. "I'm sending him my demo tape. He's going to make sure it gets heard by the right people."

"Really? That's exciting!"

From inside the house, Blossom calls us to breakfast.

"Are you hungry?" I ask.

"No. But I'll eat. She won't take *no* for an answer. And those biscuits? I'm pretty sure they've got a little slice of heaven baked inside."

I laugh out loud. "You have no idea."

"Who is she anyway?"

I smile. "Just an old friend."

When we enter the kitchen, Blossom is nowhere to be seen. But on the porch, a feast awaits us—platters of eggs, breakfast meats, and pastries on a table dressed in green gingham linens.

We sit down opposite one another, and I reach for his hand as I offer the blessing. We help ourselves to hearty portions and eat in companionable silence. I can tell something is on Nate's mind, but he'll tell me what he's thinking when he's ready.

"Gunner's the best. I couldn't have handpicked a better dad," he finally says, his fork hovering midair. "A part of me will probably always be a little sore at you for keeping him from me. But at least now I understand why." He shovels in a bite of eggs, chews, swallows. "Your sister is a piece of work. Gunner and I talked a lot these past few days. He really cared about you, Mom. If Melanie hadn't stolen him from you, he would've married you. We would've been a family."

"Maybe." I take a sip of fresh orange juice. "But there's no use crying over spilled milk." Gunner would've married me out of obligation, not love. He would've chased his music, and I would've wanted more children. It wouldn't have worked. At least that's what I tell myself—because I can't bear to think about what might have been.

"Right. I'm just glad I found him when I did." He pops a mini blueberry muffin into his mouth and looks out at the field. "This place is awesome, Mom. I can't believe you grew up here."

"Can you stay a while?"

He shakes his head. "I wish I could. But I need to get back to work."

"Then you'll have to come back when you can stay longer."

His eyes widen. "You mean . . . you're keeping it?"

I nod. "Yep. I'm selling my townhouse and moving here permanently."

"Cool! I figured since you and Melanie owned it together, you might sell it."

"She disclaimed her portion. It all belongs to me now," I say, waving my sausage link like a victory flag.

Nate grins. "Can we buy a boat?"

I chuckle. "Sure. But fair warning—I know absolutely nothing about boats. You'll have to help me shop."

"Oh, don't you worry," he says, his eyes twinkling. "I already have some ideas."

I laugh, feeling lighter than I have in days. "I bet you do."

He checks his time. "As much as I hate to leave, I really should get going."

"I understand."

We drop our plates in the sink and head out to the driveway.

"I'm coming to Richmond next week," I say, opening his car door for him. "I need to find a Realtor and put the townhouse on the market. Maybe we can grab dinner."

"Sure. Just let me know when." As he's getting into the car, he pauses, glancing down at the passenger-side floorboard. "Oh! I almost forgot." He leans over and picks something up. "This was in your stack of mail when I stopped by the townhouse. It looked important. I thought you might need it."

He hands me a manila envelope. There is no return address, but the writing is unmistakable. Mama's.

Thirty-Five

I dump the envelope's contents onto the kitchen table, and a dozen miniature cassette tapes scatter across the surface, an antiquated recording device tumbling out after it. No note. I shake the envelope, then peer inside. Nothing.

Then I notice the postmark—December 9. Mama most have mailed the package right before she died. Why did it take so long to get to me? Was it lost in the mail? I may never know the answer.

Blossom appears, as though summoned by fate. Her voice is barely above a whisper. "Is that what I think it is?"

I nod absently, gnawing on a fingernail. "It came in my mail. Mama sent it to my Richmond address—no note, no explanation. Nate brought it to me this morning. He thought it looked important."

My heart throbs as I pace, thoughts crashing into each other like waves in a storm. "How did she even get my address? Had she known where I lived this whole time but never reached out?"

Blossom doesn't respond. She's doing what she does best—listening.

"And why send them to me? Why not Mellie? Mama knew Mellie was aware of the tapes. Mellie's the one who listened to them. She knew what they were. Where they were hidden."

I stop and grip the back of a chair. "And what did she expect me to do with them? If she wanted them destroyed, she could've done that herself. But she didn't. She sent them to me. And now they're mine."

I swallow, my throat suddenly dry. "If my life wasn't in danger before, it most certainly is now. Mama would've known that. She knew the risks."

My eyes dart to the window. "Did she . . . did she do this on purpose? Did she send the Watchmen after me? Is that what this is?"

Suddenly realizing someone might be listening to us, I press a finger to my lips and motion to the back door. Scooping the tapes back into the envelope, I pass it to Blossom. Without hesitation, she slips it into her deep pocket, where it vanishes into the folds of her dress.

We slip outside and walk until we're far enough away from the house for any listening devices to pick us up. "That was careless of me. I may have just driven the last nail in my coffin."

Blossom's eyes scan the landscape. "What now? Should you call the police?"

"Not yet." I press a hand to my forehead, wishing I could physically hold the panic in place. "I have an idea. But I need to sort it out. If only I could figure out a way to make copies of the tapes. If the tapes vanish—or if I do—the truth can't vanish with them." I let out a slow breath. "But I don't know if that's even possible. That machine is ancient. Where would you find one like it?"

Blossom's mouth curves into a knowing smile. "You let me worry about the how. I've got a few gadgets tucked away that might just surprise you."

I blink at her. "You're serious?"

"I am." Her tone turns steely. "You're not in this alone, Goldie Girl. If there's a way to make copies, we'll find it. Better yet, I'll transfer the audio to a thumb drive."

I hold up two fingers. "Make two copies, please."

"You got it."

I blow a stray strand of hair off my face. "Whew! It's already been a whirlwind this morning. I'm going down to the dock to sort out my thoughts."

Blossom glances at the sky, her personal clock. "Shouldn't take me more than a couple of hours. I'll meet you down there when I'm done."

"You're the best." When I lean in to kiss her cheek, I whisper, "Be careful. If the Elders suspect we have the tapes, they'll come after us."

"I understand," she says, her demeanor more serious than I've ever seen it.

I grab my sun hat from the rack beside the front door and retreat to the solitude on the dock. I pace the weathered boards, chewing my fingernails to the nub. But the more I turn it over in my mind, the more certain I become—this plan will work. It has to. It's the only way.

I dial Cal's number, and he answers on the first ring. "I need to see you," I blurt, skipping pleasantries.

He doesn't hesitate. "I've got an errand out your way this afternoon. I'll stop in around one o'clock," he says, then ends the call.

I lower myself to the dock, leaning against a piling, forcing slow and steady breaths to calm my nerves.

This is no game. My mother has put me in a very dangerous situation.

What frustrates me more than anything else? I may never understand why.

But it's not just me. No one close to me is safe.

If Dominion is watching us, they'll know that Mellie, Nate, and Gunner were just here. We're all in danger.

Blossom arrives with a picnic basket brimming with fried chicken and all the fixings, but I'm too anxious to eat much. Sipping sweet tea, I lay out my plan. She listens intently, then nods in approval.

She pats her pocket. "I have the thumb drives. Who are they for?"

"One's for Cal, to be turned over to the authorities if anything happens to him. And the other's for me. For the same reason. I was thinking of giving mine to Arthur Pendleton, the estate attorney, for safekeeping."

"That's not necessary. I'll keep it safe for you. If something happens to you—God forbid—I'll march those tapes to every major news outlet in the country and drop them on their desks myself."

I smile, touched. "I assumed once this was over, our relationship would be too."

Blossom reaches over and squeezes my hand. "No, Goldie Girl. I will always be here if you need me." She hands me a thumb drive. "You'll want to give this one to the deputy."

I take the thumb drive from her, slipping it into my pocket as I draw in a shaky breath. "I don't know what I'll do if he doesn't agree to my plan."

Blossom rests her hand gently on my shoulder. "Don't worry. We'll think of something."

I give her a sad smile. I've already thought of everything. There is no other option.

A few minutes before one, when we hear tires on the gravel in the driveway, Blossom packs up our trash and hands me a round metal cookie tin. "Give these to the deputy," she says, her voice light, but her emerald eyes piercing. "A little birdie told me he has a thing for snickerdoodles."

I take the tin, feeling the weight of what's really inside—

her famous cookies on top, and beneath them, the original tapes that could take down Dominion.

———

Cal is skeptical when I lay out my plan. "It's too dangerous. For both of us."

"My family will always be in danger as long as the Elders think those tapes might be in my possession." I lean in close. "Do you have a contact inside Dominion? Someone higher up? An Elder or Watchman?"

He hesitates. "I have a contact. But he's not someone I trust."

"You don't have to trust him. You offer them the tapes. In exchange, they leave my family alone."

He shakes his head, eyes wide with disbelief. "It doesn't work that way, Lydia. I'm a dead man the minute I hand over the tapes. And so are you."

"That's why we have an insurance plan."

His brow lifts. "Which is?"

"I made two copies of the tapes. Thumb drives. One for you, one for me. If something happens to you—a tragic accident, an unexpected fall, a car crash—your copy will be sent to every major law enforcement agency in the country." I pause, locking eyes with him. "Do you have someone you trust with that responsibility?"

Cal nods. He doesn't have to think about it. "What about you? Do you have someone you trust?"

"I do. And if something happens to me—or anyone in my family—every major news outlet in America gets those tapes."

He exhales, visibly assessing the risk. "I don't know, Lydia. This is playing with fire."

"You told me once you want to be sheriff. That you want to follow in your father's and grandfather's footsteps. But let's be real—no one gets that job now without Dominion's blessing."

His jaw clenches. "Bribing my way into office is not what I had in mind."

"It's not a bribe. You're not taking anything from them. But if you have those tapes—if you know what they're capable of—you're not just another deputy they can control. You're the man who knows where the bodies are buried."

He looks away, considering.

"Play this right, and you'll be the one man they can't afford to cross. You'll keep your badge, earn their trust—but with leverage. You'll have real power, Cal. Not just a title. You'll get to choose what kind of sheriff you want to be. And who knows?" I add, voice softening. "You might even keep Dominion honest. Or at least less dangerous."

He exhales slowly. "All right. I'll do it."

I hand him the metal tin. "I hear you like snickerdoodles. The original tapes are tucked beneath the cookies."

A slow smile spreads across his face. "Smart hiding spot."

I reach out to shake his hand, pressing the thumb drive into his palm. "You'll need this."

The smile fades. His expression turns serious. "It's safer if I don't contact you again until after the meeting. But I'll send someone I trust to keep an eye on things here. Just in case."

"Thank you." I place a hand on his arm. "Be safe, Cal. This could change everything for both of us."

Thirty-Six

The next three hours crawl by slower than a snail trudging through molasses. Blossom and I clean like women possessed —emptying closets, scrubbing baseboards, weeding flower beds with shaky hands. Anything to keep our minds off what might be happening behind closed doors.

We're on the porch playing a jittery round of gin rummy —the setting sun casting long golden streaks across the floorboards—when Cal's patrol car crunches down the gravel drive.

My pulse quickens. "Here we go," I murmur, more to myself than Blossom.

He steps out slowly, the burden of what he's done clearly hanging from his shoulders. His campaign hat is gone. His expression is unreadable.

Blossom and I rise in unison, and I move to meet him halfway.

"It's done," he says flatly, though a sign of satisfaction tugs at his mouth. "You're better off not knowing the details. I told them you hadn't listened to the tapes, that you weren't interested in their secrets—only in peace. They bought it."

I stare at him, my heart thundering. "And you believe they'll hold up their end?"

"They gave me their word that your family will be left alone," he replies, voice low. "And I reminded them what would happen if either of us—or anyone close to you—suddenly disappears."

I fold my arms across my chest, holding back the flood of emotion. "Thank you," I whisper. "I don't know how to repay you."

"I should thank you," he says, glancing around before lowering his voice. "Dominion already sees me in a different light—like I've proven myself. Like I'm one of them. Which I'm not. But if I play this right, they'll back me when I run for sheriff. And if I win,"—his jaw tightens—"I'll start making things right from the inside. Bit by bit."

I nod, goose bumps rising along my arms. "I already feel safer just knowing you're on our side."

He gestures toward the patrol car parked across the field. "Still, just to be cautious, I've ordered round-the-clock surveillance for the next few days. If anything feels off—anything at all—you call me."

As he turns to go, the shadows stretch a little longer, the night pressing in from the edges. And for the first time, I feel like we just might survive this.

I watch Cal's patrol car retreat down the driveway, and when I turn back toward the porch, Blossom is already uncorking a bottle of champagne. I join her and she hands me a glass.

"I don't drink often, but dismantling a generations-old corrupt secret society calls for bubbles." She raises her glass in a toast. "Sweet tea won't cut it for this victory."

With a loud sigh, Blossom lowers herself to a rocker. "I want to enjoy my last sunset. I sure am going to miss this place."

"Do you have to leave so soon? Stay for a few days—at least through the weekend. As my guest. I'll pamper you. It's my turn to cook for *you*."

Blossom chuckles. "I wish I could, Goldie Girl. But I've got to be moving on. Some other lost soul out there needs my guidance. Besides, don't you already have plans for the weekend?"

I blink in confusion. Then I realize she's talking about Sam. I never told her I was hoping to make up with Sam. As with everything else, she just knows.

A mix of dread and anticipation stirs in my chest. What if Sam rejects me? I shake off the thought. I'll worry about him tomorrow. Tonight, I want to spend my last hours alone with Blossom.

"Do you know where you're going next?" I ask, sipping my champagne.

"They never tell me." She rests her head on the back of the chair. "But it won't be as lovely as Marsh Hollow. This is the closest place to heaven as I've visited on earth."

I let out a contented breath. "It's special, isn't it?"

"Mm-hmm. Are you pleased with the way things turned out?"

"Mostly. There are some questions I'll never have the answer to—like why Mama sent the evidence to me and not Mellie."

"Maybe because she trusted you'd know what to do with it. And she was right. You handled the situation beautifully."

I'll probably always wonder how long Mama had my address, and why she never reached out. But I keep those thoughts to myself. Some stories end with questions. Like a good novel that doesn't tie up every thread. You get to decide what happens next, in whatever way brings you the most peace.

"This might help with one of your loose ends," she says, pulling an envelope out of her pocket and handing it to me.

I stare at it. "What is this?"

"A brief bio and the current location for Whit Calloway. I found it online. You could've too."

I hold the envelope up to the fading sunlight, but of course, I can't see through it. "Please tell me he's not in prison."

Blossom laughs. "No, Goldie. He's not in prison. From what I read, he seems like an honorable man. He's still a horse trainer, living in Kentucky. I couldn't find any evidence of a wife or children."

I press the envelope to my chest. My father. After all these years, is it really possible?

Blossom refills our glasses, and we sit in silence, lost in our thoughts.

Eventually, I ask, "How will I reach you if I need you?"

She kisses her fingertips and presses them to my cheek. "Wish upon a star, and I'll be here in a jiffy."

Later, Blossom brings out a charcuterie board with meats and cheeses, and we nibble on it for dinner. I plan to make her a farewell breakfast, but when I wake on Saturday morning, her mini bus is gone from the yard. I smile to myself. Typical Blossom. She doesn't strike me as the tearful-goodbye type.

I spend an embarrassing amount of time deciding what to wear to see Sam. After trying on half my closet, I decide on floral capri pants and a yellow tee—simple, cheerful, and not too dressy.

My stomach's in knots as I drive the short distance to his cottage. He's mowing the grass when I arrive. At first, his expression is confused, but it quickly shifts into a broad smile. He turns off the mower and walks over to greet me. "This is a surprise."

"Long overdue. I wanted to tie up my family business

before I came to see you—to apologize. I was rude to you the day of the tornado."

He shrugs. "I guess I deserved it."

"You most certainly did not. But let's not argue over spilled milk."

He nods. "Agreed. How're things with Nate?"

I smile. "Nate's found his father, and they're building a relationship. My sister came for a visit. I wish I could say our reunion went as well."

"I'm sorry," he says with a sympathetic smile.

I wave off his concern. "Honestly, seeing Mellie through adult eyes gave me a kind of closure I didn't know I needed. I spent years clinging to this perfect version of her—the big sister who could do no wrong. But that was a child's view. Now I understand her for who she really is. Flawed. Wounded. Complicated. And for the first time, I can let go of the illusion."

"That kind of clarity doesn't come easy. It hurts, realizing someone you love isn't who you thought they were." His fingers graze the outside of my arm—a light, barely there touch that sends a ripple through me. "But there's strength in seeing the truth . . . and peace too. Even if it stings a little."

Unexpected tears blur my vision. "A lot of stinging."

Sam nudges a pebble with the toe of his boot. "So, what's next for you? Are you going back to Richmond?"

"I am. Next week." When disappointment flickers across his face, I add, "To put my townhouse on the market. I've accepted a job at Driftwood and start on June first. I'm moving to Marsh Hollow permanently."

His face lights up—the exact reaction I was hoping for. "Congratulations. I think you'll be really happy here. And I know our neighbors will be relieved a developer won't be building Cookie Cutter Cove on the property."

I laugh. "Trust me, we're all relieved." My gaze shifts to the lawnmower. "I can see you're in the middle of something, but I was wondering if you might be free later."

He tilts his head. "I'm almost done here. What did you have in mind?"

"Something outdoors, since it's such a beautiful day. Maybe . . . a picnic?"

His smile widens. "A picnic sounds perfect. I know just the place—a secluded beach. We'll have to take the boat to get there. We can sip chilled white wine and talk about nothing but happy things."

"I like that idea. No serious subjects allowed. I'll pack the picnic since you're providing the boat."

He checks his watch. "It's almost eleven. How about I pick you up around one?"

"I'll be ready."

"And wear your bathing suit," he adds with a wink. "We might want to go for a swim."

"Got it. I'll see you then."

I walk backward toward my car, not quite ready to look away from him.

He closes the distance and pulls me into a warm hug—solid and grounding, like a promise.

"I'm sorry," he says quietly, his breath warm near my ear. "For not standing by you when it mattered. I won't make that mistake again."

I lean back just enough to look at him, my hands still resting on his arms. "I'm not the same woman I was back then. Even if 'back then' was only a couple of weeks ago."

A half-smile tugs at his lips, but I press on.

"I've faced things I never thought I could. Lost some illusions. Found the truth. About my family, my past . . . myself." I pause, emotions welling. "What I need now is someone who sees me for who I really am."

He cups my elbow gently, his gaze holding mine. "I see you, Lydia. And I'm not going anywhere."

Reluctantly, I step away, letting the space return between us. We exchange one last look—something quiet and full of understanding—and I turn toward the car.

As I drive away, sunlight flickers through the trees, the road ahead wide open. For the first time in years, maybe ever, my life feels like it's headed somewhere—not just forward, but toward something beautiful.

And for once, I'm not just surviving.

I'm beginning again.

———

I hope you've enjoyed *Return to Marsh Hollow*, the first installment in the Soul Seekers collections. The books in the collection are stand alone and do not need to be read in order.

Looking for more Southern family drama? Check out my other series and trilogies: Marsh Harbor, Sandy Island, Palmetto Island, Hope Springs, and Virginia Vineyards.

Use the QR code below to access my online store where you'll find bundled series and receive early access to my new releases. Buying direct means you are supporting the artist instead of big business. I appreciate you. Ashley Farley Books

Also available at Barnes and Noble, Kobo, Apple Books, Amazon, and many other online book sellers.

Made in United States
Cleveland, OH
20 June 2025